KU-014-189

Ox-Tales
EARTH

Original stories from
remarkable writers

P

Ox-Tales are published in support of

Oxfam

First published in Great Britain in 2009 by *Green*Profile, an imprint of
Profile Books Ltd, 3A Exmouth House, Pine Street, London EC1R 0JH

COPYRIGHTS

Earth © Vikram Seth 2009; *The Jester of Astapovo* © Rose Tremain;
2009; *The Nettle Pit* © Jonathan Coe 2009; *Boys in Cars* © Marti
Leimbach 2009; *Lucky We Live Now* © Kate Atkinson 2009; *Fieldwork* ©
John Rebus Ltd 2009; *The Importance of Warm Feet* © Marina Lewycka
2009; *Long Ago Yesterday* © Hanif Kureishi 2004; *Telescope* © Jonathan
Buckley 2009; *The Death of Marat* © Nicholas Shakespeare 2009;
Afterword: Earth © Oxfam 2009.

The moral right of the authors has been asserted

All rights reserved. Without limiting the rights under copyright
reserved above, no part of this publication may be reproduced, stored
or introduced into a retrieval system, or transmitted, in any form or
by any means (electronic, mechanical, photocopying, recording or
otherwise), without the prior written permission of both the copyright
owner and the publisher of this book.

Printed in the UK by CPI Bookmarque, Croydon, CR0 4TD
Typeset in Iowan to a design by Sue Lamble

1 3 5 7 9 10 8 6 4 2

A CIP catalogue record for this book is
available from the British Library
ISBN: 978 1 84668 258 2

© **Mixed Sources**
Product group from well-managed
forests and other controlled sources
www.fsc.org Cert no. TT-COC-002227
FSC © 1996 Forest Stewardship Council

Ox-Tales: Earth

OX-TALES: EARTH is one of four original collections, featuring stories by leading British- and Irish-based writers. Each of the writers has contributed their story for free in order to raise money and awareness for Oxfam. The FOUR ELEMENTS provide a loose framework for the stories and highlight key areas of Oxfam's work: water projects (WATER), aid for conflict areas (FIRE), agricultural development (EARTH), and action on climate change (AIR). An afterword, at the end of each book, explains how Oxfam makes a difference. And in buying this book, you'll be a part of that process, too.

Compiling these books, we asked authors for new stories; or, from novelists who don't do short stories, work in progress from their next book. The response was thirty-eight original pieces of fiction, which are spread across the four books and framed by a cycle of element poems by Vikram Seth. We think they're extraordinary, but be your own judge. And if you like what you read here, please buy all four OX-TALES books – and help Oxfam work towards an end to poverty worldwide.

Mark Ellingham (Profile) & Peter Florence (Hay Festival)
Editors, OX-TALES

Acknowledgments

The Ox-Tales books were developed at Profile Books by Mark Ellingham in association with Peter Florence and Hay Festival. Thanks from us both to the authors who contributed stories – and time – to creating these four collections in support of Oxfam. And thanks, too, to their publishers and agents who, without exception, offered generous support to this project.

At Oxfam, Tom Childs has guided the project alongside Suzy Smith, Charlie Hayes, Annie Lewis, Fee Gilfeather, Annemarie Papatheofilou and Matt Kurton.

At Profile, Peter Dyer, Penny Daniel, Niamh Murray, Duncan Clark, Claire Beaumont, Simon Shelmerdine, Ruth Killick, Rebecca Gray, Kate Griffin and Andrew Franklin have been instrumental. Thanks also to Nikky Twyman and Caroline Pretty for proofreading, and to Jonathan Gray for his cover illustrations.

Contents

VIKRAM SETH (born Calcutta, India, 1952) is the author of the novels *The Golden Gate* (1986), *A Suitable Boy* (1993) and *An Equal Music* (1999), and of books of poetry, travel, fable and memoir.

'Earth' is part of a sequence of poems, *Seven Elements*, incorporating the elements in the European, Indian and Chinese traditions (earth, air, fire, water, wood, metal and space). Set to music by the composer Alec Roth, *Seven Elements* will be performed in summer 2009 at the Salisbury, Chelsea and Lichfield festivals.

Earth

Here in this pot lies soil,
In which all things take birth.
The blind roots curve and coil
White in the sunless earth.
The soil slips over fire.
The great lands crack apart
And lava, pulsing higher,
Springs from earth's molten heart.

Here in this jar lies clay,
Dried clay, a whitened dust.
The moistened fingers play
To make it what they must.
The earth begins to reel,
Round, round, and near and far,
And on the potter's wheel
Is born another jar.

Here in this urn lies ash,
Dust uninfused with breath:
Burnt wood, burnt bone, burnt flesh,
The powdered clay of death.
The embers from the pyre
Sink on the rivered earth
And moistened into mire
Wait for a further birth.

Vikram Seth

The Jester of Astapovo

ROSE TREMAIN (born London, 1943) lives in London and Norfolk, with the biographer Richard Holmes. Her books have won many prizes: *Restoration* (1989) was shortlisted for the Booker Prize and made into a film and a stage play; *Sacred Country* (1992) won the James Tait Black Memorial Prize and the Prix Fémina Etranger; *Music and Silence* (1999) won the Whitbread Novel Award; and *The Road Home* (2007), her most recent book, won the Orange Prize for Fiction.

A FEW WEEKS BEFORE the main events of this story disturbed forever the life of its protagonist, Ivan Andreyevich Ozolin, he had believed himself to be in love with an older woman, Tanya Trepova.

The year was 1910. Ivan Andreyevich Ozolin was the stationmaster of Astapovo, an insignificant little stop some 120 miles south-east of Moscow, on the Smolensk–Dankovo section of the Ural railroad line. He was forty-six and had been married to his wife, Anna Borisovna Ozolina, for twenty years. Tanya Trepova was a widow of fifty-three with excellent deportment, but whose pale face wore an expression of perpetual and affecting melancholy. It had been this melancholy of hers that Ivan Ozolin had longed to alleviate. On one of his days off (which were few) he arranged to go on a bicycling trip to the forest with Tanya Trepova, pretending to Anna Borisovna that he was going mushroom picking.

Ivan Ozolin and Tanya Trepova sat down on the mossy earth, where there were indeed a few pale mushrooms nestling among the tree roots. Ivan wanted to lean over and kiss Tanya, but he felt that to touch with his lips features still set in such a sorrowful arrangement was tantamount to an insult. So what he decided to do was to lean back on his elbows and cross one leg over the other and point out to his would-be mistress the ridiculous appearance of his white cycling socks.

'Look at these!' he said with a guffaw. 'And look at the little bit of my leg showing between the top of the sock and the bottom of my trousers. How can we take anything seriously – anything in the world – when we catch sight of things like this? Life's a joke, don't you think so, Tanya? Every single thing in life is a joke – except love.'

A smile did now appear on Tanya Trepova's face. It remained there long enough for Ivan to get up the courage to say: 'I'd like to make you happy. I'm serious about that. My wife thinks I'm a fool who jokes about everything, but to jest is better than to despair, don't you think?'

The September sun, coming and going between clouds, flickering through the trees, now suddenly laid on Tanya Trepova's pale skin a steady and warming light. But as soon as this light arrived there, her smile vanished and she said: 'Sometimes despair is unavoidable.'

Then she got to her feet and brushed down her skirt and said: 'I shouldn't have come to the forest with you, Ivan Andreyevich. I can't think what I was doing. I only agreed because I was flattered by the kind attention you've shown me since my husband died, and because I enjoy cycling. But please let's go back now.'

Ivan was a courteous man. Despite his strong feelings for Tanya Trepova, he wasn't the type to take advantage of any woman – even here, in the eternal silence of the woods.

So he got up obediently, tugging down his trouser leg over his rucked white sock, and he and Tanya Trepova walked to where their bicycles were parked and then rode back to Astapovo, side by side, talking only of inconsequential things.

When Ivan Ozolin got home to his red-painted station-master's cottage, Anna Borisovna asked: 'Where are the mushrooms, then?'

'Oh,' said Ivan, swearing silently at his forgetfulness, 'I couldn't find any. I searched and searched. I didn't find a single one.'

Anna Borisovna stared accusingly at her husband. After twenty years of childless living with him, he wearied her. Was this just another of his stupid jokes?

'It's September and the sun's out after the long rains we've endured and there are no mushrooms in the forest?'

'No. Or perhaps there were mushrooms, but other people gathered them before I got there.'

'I don't believe you,' she said.

In October, winter began to close in on Astapovo, as it did at this time each year.

Ivan Ozolin supervised the cleaning and oiling of the ancient snowplough kept in a dilapidated shed on a siding on the Smolensk side of the tracks. He chopped wood for the pot-bellied stoves that heated his own cottage, the two waiting rooms (ladies' and gentlemen's) and the station buffet on the Dankovo side. His mind, as he went about these familiar tasks, was preoccupied by his failed attempt to have a love affair with Tanya Trepova. Most men that he knew had love affairs and even boasted about them. But he, Ivan Ozolin, hadn't been able to manage even this! It was laughable. Ivan Ozolin thought, My life's at a standstill. Trains come and go, come and go past my door day and night, but I live without moving at a way-station where nothing stops for long or endures – except the monotony of all that's already here.

The idea that this state of affairs would just go on and on and nothing important would ever happen to him ever again began to terrify him. One evening, he deliberately got drunk with his old friend Dmitri Panin, who worked in the one-man telegraph office at Astapovo station, and began to pour out his heart to him.

'Dmitri,' he said. 'How on earth are we meant to escape from the meaninglessness of life? Tell me your method.'

'My method?' said Dmitri. 'What method? I'm just a telegraph operator. I send out other people's messages and get messages back ...'

'So, you're in touch with the wider world.'

'I may be in touch with the wider world, but I don't have any message of my own. Life has not ... Life has not ... equipped me with one.'

'Equipped you? Have another drink, my friend. I think we're both talking drivel, but it seems to me there are four ways and only four ways of escaping it.'

'Escaping what?'

'Meaninglessness. The first is ignorance. I mean the ignorance of youth, when you haven't seen it yet.'

'Seen what?'

'Death waiting for you. Inevitably waiting. You know?'

Dmitri said that he knew perfectly well and that meanwhile he'd order them another bottle of vodka and a piece of special Smolenski sausage to keep them from falling under the table. Then he asked Ivan Ozolin to hurry through the other 'three ways of escape' because he had a feeling that they were going to bore him or depress him, or both.

Ivan gulped more vodka. He tried to explain to Dmitri Panin that, in his view, human beings were just merely 'randomly united lumps of matter'. Some people, such as his wife, Anna Borisovna, refuted this and believed that human life had been created by God. 'She thinks', said Ivan Ozolin, 'that, contrary to all evidence, God is benign … but me, I can't go along—'

'Yes, yes,' said Dmitri. 'We know all that twaddle and counter-twaddle. Come on, Ivan, let's change the subject. Let's talk about Tanya Trepova, for instance.'

Ivan Ozolin scratched his head, balding on the crown, growing sensitive to winter cold.

He didn't really want to talk about Tanya Trepova, even to Dmitri. He began cutting up the hunk of Smolenski sausage into manageable pieces.

'That was a farce,' he said.

'A farce?'

'Yes. I didn't even kiss her.' And then he let out one of his famous guffaws of laughter.

Dmitri began to cram his face with sausage. 'I can't see what's so funny about that,' he said with his mouth full. 'If it had been me, I would have kissed her, at least.'

On the afternoon of 31st October, a cold day marked by an icy wind and flurries of snow, a southbound train from

Tula arrived at Astapovo station. Ivan Ozolin, wearing his stationmaster's uniform, was standing alone on the platform, holding his flags, waiting to see if anybody was going to disembark before waving his green flag to send the train onwards towards Dankovo. He saw the door of one of the second-class carriages open and a young woman stepped down and came towards him.

She was plump, with a wide, homely face, and wore a peasant scarf over her brown hair.

'Stationmaster!' she called. 'We need your help. Please. You must help us ...'

Ivan Ozolin hurried towards her. Her voice, he noticed at once, was not the voice of a peasant.

'What can I do?' said Ivan.

'My father is on the train. We were trying to get to Dankovo, but he's been taken ill, very ill. A doctor is with us. The doctor says we must get off here and find a bed for my father. Or he could die. Please can you help us?'

Ivan Ozolin now saw that the young woman was trembling violently, whether with cold or agitation, or both, and he knew that at all costs he would have to do whatever he could to help her and her sick father; it was his duty as a stationmaster and as a human being.

He followed her to the open door of the second-class carriage. Steam billowed all around them in the freezing air.

He climbed aboard the train and was led along the crowded carriage to one of the hard leather benches where an elderly man was lying, covered by a thin blanket. By his side knelt the doctor, wearing a black coat. From all the other benches passengers were staring and whispering.

'Dushan,' the young woman said to the doctor. 'Here's the stationmaster. Between the two of you, you can carry Papa to the waiting room and then this good man is going to find us a bed for him, aren't you, sir?'

'A bed? Yes, of course …'

'There's an inn here, I suppose? What's this place called?'

'Astapovo.'

'Astapovo. I've never heard of it, have you, Dushan? But everywhere has some little inn or hotel. Hasn't it?'

Her agitation was growing all the time. He saw that she could hardly bear to look down at her father, so greatly did the sight of him lying there in his blanket upset her. Very calmly, Ivan Ozolin said: 'There is no inn in Astapovo. But the fact that there is no inn in Astapovo doesn't mean that there are no beds. We can arrange a bed for your father in my cottage … just over there on the Smolensk side of the track … that red house you can glimpse …'

'Dushan,' said the young woman, now breaking down into tears, 'he says there's no inn. What are we going to do?'

The doctor stood up. He put a comforting arm round the young woman's shoulders and held out his other hand to Ivan Ozolin. 'I am Doctor Dushan Makovitsky,' he said. 'Please tell me your name, stationmaster.'

Ivan Ozolin took Makovitsky's hand and shook it. He bowed. 'I am Ivan Andreyevich Ozolin, doctor,' he said.

'Very well,' said Makovitsky. 'Now let me explain the situation. My patient here is Count Tolstoy: Leo Nikolayevich Tolstoy, the world-famous writer. He was attempting to get as far as Novocherkassk, to stay with his sister, but he has been taken ill. I'm desperately afraid he may have pneumonia. Will you help us to save his life?'

Leo Tolstoy …

Ivan Ozolin felt his mouth drop foolishly open. He looked down at the old man, who was clutching in his frail hands a small embroidered cushion, much as a child clutches to itself a beloved toy. For a moment, he found himself unable to speak, but could only repeat to himself: Leo Tolstoy has come to Astapovo … Then he managed to pull himself together sufficiently to say: 'I'll do everything I can, doctor. Everything in my power. Luckily the waiting rooms are on this side of the track, so we haven't got far to carry him.'

Dushan Makovitsky bent down and gently lifted Tolstoy's shoulders. The old man's eyes opened suddenly and he began murmuring the words: 'Escape … I have to escape …'

His daughter stroked his head. 'We're moving you, Papa,' she said. 'We're going to find you a warm bed.'

Ivan Ozolin took hold of the writer's legs, noting that underneath the blanket, he was wearing peasant clothes: a tunic tied at the waist, moleskin trousers tucked into worn boots. When the two men lifted him up, Ivan was surprised at how light his body felt. He was a tall man, but with very little flesh on his bones.

They carried him gently from the train and out into the snow. Feeling the snowflakes touch his face, Leo Tolstoy said: 'Ah, it comes round me now. The cold of the earth …'

But the distance to the waiting room wasn't very great and soon enough Dr Makovitsky and Ivan Ozolin had lain the elderly writer down on a wooden bench near the wood-burning stove. Instructing the doctor to go back to the train for their bags, Tolstoy's daughter did her best to make her father comfortable on the bench, tucking the blanket round him, taking the little pillow from his hands and placing it gently under his head, smoothing his springy white beard.

Ivan hovered there a moment. His heart was beating wildly. He explained that he had an immediate duty to supervise the train's onward departure towards Dankovo, but as soon as this was done, he would run to his cottage

THE JESTER OF ASTAPOVO

and prepare a bed for Count Tolstoy. 'My wife will help me,' he said. 'It will be an honour.'

The cottage had only four rooms: a living room, a kitchen, a bedroom and a small office where Ivan Ozolin kept his railway timetables and his stationmaster's log. Outside the cottage was a vegetable garden and a privy.

When Ivan Ozolin came rushing in to tell Anna Borisovna that Leo Tolstoy, gravely ill, had arrived to Astapovo and needed a bed in their house, she was boiling laundry on the kitchen range. She turned and stared at her husband. 'Is this another of your jokes?' she asked.

'No,' said Ivan. 'On the soul of my mother, this is not one of my jokes. We must give up our bed, Anna. To the poor and needy of this land, Tolstoy is a saint. In the name of all those who suffer today in Russia, we must make our own small sacrifice!'

Anna Borisovna, though tempted to mock the sudden floweriness of Ivan's language (brought on, no doubt, by the unexpected arrival of a famous writer), refrained from doing so, and together she and Ivan went to their room and began dismantling their iron bed. The bed was heavy and old and the bolts rusty, and this work took them the best part of half an hour.

They carried the bed into their sitting room and reassembled it, dragged their mattress on to it and then laid on clean sheets and pillow cases and woollen blankets from their blanket chest. While Ivan banked up the stove, Anna set a night table by the bed and a chamber pot underneath it. She put a jug of water and a bowl and some linen towels on the night table. She said to Ivan: 'I wish I had some violets to put in a little vase for him.'

'Never mind that,' said Ivan Ozolin. 'Now you must come with me and we'll carry him across the tracks. Only twenty-nine minutes before the Dankovo train.'

When they got back to the waiting room, Tolstoy was sleeping. His daughter, too, had gone to sleep kneeling on the hard floor, with her head lying on the bench, near her father's muddy boots. Dushan Makovitsky kept a lonely vigil at their side and seemed very relieved to see Ivan return with Anna Borisovna.

'Good people,' he said in a whisper. 'You can't know how grateful I am. You must understand that this is a terrible business. Terrible beyond imagining. Count Tolstoy left his home in secret two nights ago. He left because his wife had made his life unbearable. He left to try to find peace, far away from the Countess. But he lives in mortal fear of being followed, of his whereabouts being discovered by her. So secrecy is vital. You understand? Nobody but you must know that he's here.'

Ivan and Anna nodded. Ivan murmured that of course they understood, and would respect the need for concealment. But he nevertheless felt himself go cold with sudden terror. He looked down at the old man. Surely he – who must by now be in his eighties – would have preferred to live out his last years peacefully on his estates, and yet he'd run away in the middle of an October night! What marital persecutions had pushed him to make this extraordinary decision? If this was what marriage had done to someone as wise as Leo Tolstoy – to the author of *War and Peace* and *Anna Karenina* – what might it eventually do to him, the humble stationmaster of Astapovo?

He glanced up at the waiting room clock. Seventeen minutes remained before the arrival of the Dankovo train.

'We should hurry,' he said. 'Everything is prepared.'

Now, as darkness came down, the great writer Leo Tolstoy was undressed tenderly by his daughter, who put a clean nightshirt on him and combed his hair and beard and helped him to lie down in the iron bed. He was very tired and weak, but he knew that he was in a strange place and Ivan and Anna, working next door in their small kitchen, heard him say to his daughter: 'Sasha, I know I'm ill. I suppose I could be dying. So I want you to send a telegram to Vladimir Chertkov and ask him to come here. Send it tonight.'

'Yes, all right, Papa. But if Mama finds out that you sent for Chertkov and not for her—'

'I can't help it. To see her face would kill me! I can't set eyes on her ever again. I can't. But I must see Chertkov. There's all the wretched business of my will and my copyrights to settle …'

'All of that was sorted out, Father. Vladimir and I know your wishes; that all the copyrights are willed to me and I authorise that your works are to be made available to the Russian people, free of any charge …'

'Yes. But Vladimir is to be the executor. Only him. Not you, not Tanya, not any of my good-for-nothing sons. Vladimir Chertkov alone will decide what's to be published and by whom and when … both the fiction and all the other work … and the diaries your mother tried to steal …'

'He knows. You've been through it a hundred times.'

'No, we haven't been through it a hundred times. And I want him here, Sasha! Don't argue with me! Arguments give me a pain in my heart. Where's Dushan?'

'Dushan's sleeping, Papa. In the waiting room. He hasn't slept for thirty hours …'

Then, as Ivan and Anna tugged out their few pieces of good china and Anna began to wash these, they heard the sound of wailing and it reminded them both of the noise that a wolf can make when it finds its leg caught in a trap. Ivan stared helplessly at his wife. He wished he could summon up some terrible joke to crack, as a weapon against the wolf-howls coming from next door, but he just couldn't think of one.

'Try to stop crying, Papa,' they heard Sasha say. 'It really does no good. I'm going to send the telegram to Vladimir now. Then I'll be back and we'll see whether you can eat something.'

The front door of their cottage opened and closed. The Ozolins knew they were alone in their house with Leo Tolstoy. They thought of the long night ahead, with no bed to sleep on. But it was almost time for the 5.18 train from Tula, so Ivan Ozolin tugged on his overcoat and gloves and took down his red and green flags and went out by the back door. Anna Borisovna dried the china slowly. After a few minutes, she heard the weeping diminish, breath by breath, as though the weeper had just become exhausted with it.

The following morning, under a blank grey sky, Vladimir Chertkov arrived on the 9.12 train from Moscow. He was a good-looking man in his fifties with a well-trimmed brown

beard. When Sasha greeted Chertkov on the Dankovo platform, Ivan Ozolin heard him say: 'Where in heaven's name
have I come to? There's nothing here.'

They had to wait for the Dankovo-bound train to leave
before they could cross the tracks to the cottage. Ivan Ozolin
had hoped to accompany them. He felt that, at last, his own
life was bound up with something important and he didn't
want to miss a moment of it. But when the steam from
the departed train cleared, he saw that Sasha and Chertkov
were already walking away from him over the rails, so he
stood there and let them go, while he slowly folded up his
green flag.

Then he caught sight of Dmitri Panin running in an agi-
tated way along the Smolensk platform, waving a telegram in
his hand. As Chertkov and Sasha passed him, Dmitri stopped
and hesitated, but then hurried on to the end of the platform
and began beckoning frantically to Ivan Ozolin. In the sunless morning, Dmitri's face appeared as red as a beet.

'Look at this!' he gasped, when Ivan reached him. 'It's
from Countess Tolstoy – to her husband! What in the world
is going on?'

Ivan seized the telegram and read: *We know where you are.
Arriving with Andrei, Ilya, Tanya and Mikhail tonight. Special
Pullman train from Tula. Signed: Your loyal wife, Countess Sonya
Andreyevna Tolstoya.*

'Ivan,' said Dmitri. 'Tell me what the hell is happening ...'

'All right, all right,' said Ivan. 'It's too late for secrecy now, if she knows where he is.'

'But how did she find out? You didn't send a message, did you?'

'Me? Message to who?'

'Somebody must have sent a message. How could it have got out except via your telegraph office?'

Dmitri wiped a hand across his sweating brow. 'Ivan,' he said, 'I haven't the faintest idea what you're talking about!'

'Oh, the poor man ...' murmured Ivan. 'He said he'll die, if he catches sight of her!'

'What? Who will die?'

'Count Tolstoy. He's here, Dmitri.'

'Here? What d'you mean? Here, where?'

'In my bed. No, keep your hair on, it isn't one of my jests. I swear. Leo Tolstoy is here, in the bed of the stationmaster of Astapovo! Now, give me back the telegram. I'd better give someone this news.'

When Ivan Ozolin went into the dark living room of the cottage, he saw by the soft candlelight a scene which reminded him of a religious picture. Leo Tolstoy was lying, propped up on the white pillows, with his white hair and beard fanning out from his face like a frosty halo. Leaning towards him, one on either side of him, were his daughter Sasha and his friend and faithful secretary, Vladimir Chertkov. Their heads rested tenderly against Tolstoy's shoulders. They stroked his hands, clasping the embroidered cushion, with theirs. Sasha's dark hair was loose and spread over her blue blouse. The Madonna, thought Ivan. The Madonna (just a little plump) with St John, at the foot of the Cross ...

Though he hesitated to interrupt this beautiful scene of adoration – particularly with news he imagined would be so unwelcome – he knew that he had to warn someone about the arrival of the Countess. Luckily, when Tolstoy saw him come in, he said: 'Oh my friends, here is the good man, Ivan Andreyevich Ozolin, who has been so very kind to us. Come here, stationmaster, and let me introduce you to my most beloved friend, Vladimir Chertkov.'

Chertkov stood up and Ivan Ozolin shook his hand. 'Thank you for all you've done,' Chertkov said. 'We fervently hope the Count will soon be well enough to travel onwards, but in the meantime ...'

'Sir,' said Ivan. 'Anything we've been able to do for Count Tolstoy ... it's done from deep in our hearts.

But I wonder whether I might have a word with you in private?'

Chertkov followed Ivan out into the cold, closing the door behind them, and they walked a little way from the window of the living room and stood by the fence that bordered the vegetable garden. Looking distractedly down at the carrots, onions and leeks in their little rows, Ivan passed the telegram to Chertkov and heard his gasp of horror as he took in the news of the Countess's arrival.

'Disaster!' said Chertkov. 'God in heaven, how could she have known?'

Ivan shook his head. 'I asked my telegraph man, Dmitri Panin, if anything had gone from here and he swore ...'

'No, no. I'm not suggesting you were in any way ... Oh, but you can't know, stationmaster, what a fiend that woman is! Mad with jealousy. Prying among the Count's papers and diaries day and night. Threatening suicide. Never giving him any peace ... And now ... This is going to kill him!'

At this moment Dr. Dushan Makovitsky came over the tracks, from where he'd been taking breakfast in the small buffet which served dry little meals to the few travellers who boarded or left trains at Astapovo. When news of the arrival of the Countess was conveyed to Makovitsky, he remained calm. 'The solution is simple,' he said. 'We'll say nothing to Leo Nikolayevich. We'll just close the doors to the cottage – front and back – we'll close them and lock them and neither Countess Tolstoy nor any of her other children will be allowed in.'

'So we're going to be locked in?' said Anna Borisovna to Ivan that afternoon, as she toiled over her bread-baking. 'This is getting stupid. We've given up our bed. Now we're going to be prisoners, are we?'

Ivan looked at his wife. He noticed, as if for the first time, how grey and straggly her hair appeared. He wondered how it would look – and how he would cope with the way it looked – when she was old.

'Well, or you could get on a train and leave, Anna Borisovna,' he said. 'Perhaps Countess Tolstoy would let you take her private Pullman back to Tula?'

'That's not funny,' said Anna Borisovna. 'Nothing you say is funny any more.'

Ivan Ozolin smiled. 'Jokes need the right audiences,' he said. 'A joke is a contract with another human being.'

As Anna turned away from him, they both heard a new sound coming from next door, the sound of hiccups. They heard Tolstoy cry out for Chertkov and then for Dushan Makovitsky. They waited. The hiccups continued, very loud.

Tolstoy now called out for Sasha, but no consoling voice was heard.

'They must be asleep,' said Ivan. 'Somewhere.'

'Well, and that's another thing,' hissed Anna. 'Just where in the world are all these new arrivals going to be housed? Are you expecting them to sleep under the telegraph counter with Dmitri?'

'Yes,' said Ivan. 'I was thinking that would be convenient. That way they're on hand to send telegrams to the press bureaus of the world.'

Anna Borisovna seized a dishcloth covering a bowl of yeast and snapped it angrily in her husband's face, stinging his cheek. He put his hand to his face. He wanted to retaliate by pulling her dishevelled hair, pulling it until it hurt, but he stopped himself.

He didn't want to become the kind of pig who beat his wife. He didn't want to become a pig at all. He was enjoying his role as the 'saviour' of Leo Tolstoy's life and he didn't want that disturbed.

He was on the platform, with Sasha and Dr Makovitsky, when the gleaming Pullman arrived. Once Countess Tolstoy and her four eldest children had descended and had been led into the ladies' waiting room by Sasha,

Ivan Ozolin, as instructed by Chertkov, told the driver
of the Pullman to shunt the two carriages into the siding
running parallel with the Dankovo track and leave them
there.

He then went into the waiting room. He found the
Countess weeping in Sasha's arms and the other grown-
up children standing around with faces set in expressions
of grumpy disdain. When the Countess raised her head to
acknowledge his presence, he saw a fleshy face, every part
of which appeared swollen, whether by grief or malady or
gourmandise he was unable to say.

'So it's you!' she said, flinging out an accusing gloved
finger. 'It's you who are hiding him!'

'Hush, Mama,' said Sasha.

'You should know', said the Countess to Ivan, 'that,
wherever my husband goes, I go too. If he's in your bed,
then that is where I am going to sleep!'

She broke again into a storm of weeping, which only
calmed a little when Anna Borisovna came into the waiting
room with a tray of hot tea and some slices of cinnamon
cake, which everybody fell upon. It was now near to mid-
night. Dr Makovitsky drew Ivan aside.

'Are the Pullman cars staying here?' he asked.

'Yes,' Ivan was able to say. 'But I think the train company
is going to levy a charge.'

'Friend,' said Makovitsky, 'in any crisis, there are always roubles to pay.'

All night, Leo Tolstoy coughed and hiccuped. At around three o'clock, Sasha woke Anna and Ivan and asked if some infusion could be made to relieve these sufferings.

They staggered, exhausted, to the kitchen and put water on to boil and took down jars of dried sage and comfrey and cloves. 'How much longer is this going to go on?' asked Anna.

Ivan carried the infusion into the living room, which was very dark, the candles having burnt low. He laid the jug down on the cluttered night table. Vladimir Chertkov, in his nightshirt, was lying across the end of Tolstoy's bed. Dr Makovitsky was taking the old man's pulse. The great writer was curled up in the bed, seeming small like a child. Ivan glimpsed blood on his pillow.

'Escape …' he was heard to murmur once again. 'I must escape …'

Ivan Ozolin rose early to see in the 7.12 from Moscow via Tula to Dankovo.

In the normal way, perhaps two or three passengers got

off, or the train crew changed here. But this morning, every single door all the way down the train opened and fifty or sixty people disembarked.

Ivan Ozolin stared at this crowd. Perhaps he'd known they'd come eventually, that the life of Leo Tolstoy was as precious to the people of his country as the earth itself and that, if he was going to die, they would want some part in his dying. He could see straight away that many of the arrivals were newsmen with cameras, and as they milled around on the platform – looking in vain for some grand Station Hotel or the presence of a commodious telegraph office – he felt himself surrender to them, to the grand circus that was accumulating at Astapovo. He wanted to embrace them, to say, 'You were right to come! Life is un-eventful, my friends! Don't I know it! But here's an event: the dying Tolstoy trying to keep his wife at bay! So come and get your bit of it and remember forever whatever you think it teaches you.'

Now, the two waiting rooms, the station buffet, the two Pullman cars and the freezing anteroom that adjoined Dmitri Panin's telegraph office were crammed with report-ers, all trying to buy food, send messages, write copy and above all to catch a glimpse of the writer, as he lay gasping and hiccuping in Ivan Ozolin's iron bed. Dmitri, made faint by cigarette smoke, noise and rudeness, struggled on at his post. To the front of his guichet Ivan Ozolin stuck a notice that read: *Your Telegraph Operator has not read the works of L.N. Tolstoy, so please do not waste time by asking him any questions about them.*

More journalists arrived by every train. And then from across the surrounding countryside, as the news spread, peasant farmers, blacksmiths, carpenters, laundresses, wheelwrights, slaughterers, seamstresses, milkmaids and bricklayers began to converge on Astapovo. These last slept out in the open, or in hay barns, made fires in the fields, seeming not to mind cold or hunger. A cohort of sausage-makers did a brisk trade. Potatoes were dug up by hand and roasted in the fires. Snatches of the patriotic song 'Eternal Memory' floated out across the dark earth. Normal existence was put to one side. Astapovo was where life had paused.

Chertkov ordered that the windows of Ivan's cottage be boarded up from inside. Though, with every hour, Leo Tolstoy was growing weaker, his determination not to let his wife come near him never faltered. While reporters came and went from the Pullman cars, where the Countess was giving interviews, Sasha, Makovitsky and Chertkov kept round-the-clock guard at the door of the cottage. Anna

Borisovna worked tirelessly in the kitchen, making soups and vegetable stews bulked out with barley, to feed the exhausted household.

Then, on the morning of 4th November, after Ivan Ozolin had despatched the early train to Smolensk, he turned to go back to his cottage and saw the unmistakable figure of Countess Tolstoy making her way towards his door. Behind her came several press reporters, some of them carrying cameras. Ivan Ozolin followed.

Countess Tolstoy beat on the front door of the cottage with her fists. 'Sasha!' she cried. 'Let me in!'

Ivan couldn't hear whether any reply came from inside. He watched the Countess lay her head against the door. 'Open up!' she wailed. 'Have pity, Sasha! Let people at least *believe* I've been with him!'

Still the door didn't move. The photographers jostled to get pictures of Countess Tolstoy begging to see her dying husband and being refused. But then Ivan saw his wife, who had been pegging out washing in the vegetable garden, approach the distraught woman and take her arm and lead her gently round towards the back of the house.

Anna Borisovna had a back-door key. The posse of journalists followed the two women, clumping along the little path beside the privy. And it was at this moment that Ivan Ozolin discovered the role that destiny had kept up its sleeve: he was going to be Leo Tolstoy's bodyguard!

He ran to the front door. His hands were shaking as he let himself in. He called out to Chertkov and Makovitsky: 'She's coming in the back door! My wife has a key!'

The two men rushed out into the hallway, but Ivan was the first at the door. He caught a momentary glimpse of his wife, with the Countess at her shoulder. He just had time to execute a formal bow before he slammed his weight against the door to close it in their faces. Chertkov and Makovitsky now joined him to hold the door shut. Ivan reached up and slid an iron bolt into its housing. He heard his wife crying out: 'This isn't fair! You men! We slave for you and you keep us out of your hearts!' He could hear the growl of the pressmen, pushing and questioning outside in the cold day.

'Well done, Ozolin,' said Chertkov.

'Yes, well done,' said Makovitsky. 'You may have saved his life.'

That night, as they lay on their hard floor, trying to sleep, Anna said: 'Countess Tolstoy says he's only doing this to draw attention to himself.'

'What?' said Ivan. 'Dying, d'you mean? I must try that some time when I want to get your attention.'

She turned away from him. She tugged a cushion under her shoulder.

He was up early the following day for the Tula train. A priest with an impressive beard alighted from the train and came towards him. 'I'm here to save Tolstoy's soul,' he said. 'Am I in the right place?'

'I don't know,' said Ivan. 'I thought Leo Tolstoy had been excommunicated many years ago.'

The priest was old but had lively, glittering eyes. 'The Church can punish,' he said, 'but it can also forgive.'

'Follow me,' said Ivan Ozolin. Then he added: 'My wife is a church-goer, but I am ... well, I think I'm nothing. I'm just a stationmaster.'

The priest didn't smile. As they crossed the tracks, he said: 'To be a stationmaster is not enough for a man's soul.'

'Erm ... well, I don't know,' said Ivan Ozolin. 'I've thought a lot about that. You see, I think I bring quite a fair bit of gladness to the world – just by existing. When people on the trains catch sight of me in my uniform, on the freezing platforms, they say to themselves: "Look at that poor idiot, with his red and green flags. At least we're not stuck in this nowhere of Astapovo! We have destinations!"'

'But you have none,' said the priest.

'On the contrary,' said Ozolin. 'I have one. I understand it now. My destination is here.'

The priest fared no better than Countess Tolstoy. Nobody inside the cottage would open the door to him and he had to be housed in the Pullman with, by now, so many people aboard the two carriages that the luggage racks were being used as hammocks and the on-board commode was full to overflowing.

And, in the iron bed in Ivan Ozolin's living room, the last hours of Tolstoy's life began to slip slowly by. His temperature wavered between 102.5 and 104. He was unconscious most of the time, yet bouts of hiccuping still tormented him. It grew very dark in the room, owing to a shortage of candles. In this fetid darkness, Ivan Ozolin was asked to come and prop up the bed itself, where one of the bolts had sheered off, under the weight of 'holy family' constantly sitting or leaning on the mattress. All he could find to use was a pile of bricks and he inserted these laboriously one by one, as the patient cried out in his sleep. Ice from the bricks melted and formed a pool on the floor, not far from where the chamber pot had been placed. Ivan snapped out a handkerchief and hastily mopped up the ice-water. There were, he thought, confusions enough in everybody's hearts without adding others of a domestic nature.

'When will it be over?' Anna Borisovna asked for the third or fourth time. 'When will we be free?'

'When he decides,' replied Ivan breezily. 'Writers make up their own endings.'

It came at last. On the early morning of Sunday November 7th, Countess Tolstoy was permitted to come into the sick-room – but not to approach the bed. She sat in a rocking chair, vigorously rocking and praying, with her older children clustered round her, scowling in the half-light. Sasha begged her to rock and pray more quietly, in case the patient suddenly awoke to find her there. But the patient heard nothing. And at 6.05 Dushan Makovitsky noted the final cessation of Tolstoy's breath.

The children wept – not only Sasha, but the grumpy ones as well. Vladimir Chertkov tried not to weep, but was unable to hold back his tears. Dr Makovitsky closed the dead man's eyes and folded his arms across his chest. The Countess lay her head on the blood-stained pillow and howled.

And then the great cavalcade began slowly to depart from Astapovo. As the reporters queued up at Dmitri's office to send their last messages, an engine was once again joined to the Pullman cars and the locomotive took the body of Leo Nikolayevich Tolstoy away. To wave off the Pullman with his green flag, Ivan had to push through a pungent throng of peasants, present to the last, singing 'Eternal Memory', with their arms raised in a passionate farewell and their faces blank with sorrow.

When the train had finally gone, Ivan Ozolin felt very tired and yet strangely triumphant, as though he himself had achieved victory over something that had always eluded him. He wanted to savour this victory for a little while, so he went into the now deserted station buffet and ordered a tot of vodka and a slice of cinnamon cake and sat at one of the tables with his eyes closed and his heart beating with a steady and beautiful rhythm. He knew there were many tasks still to be done; he shouldn't remain sitting like this for long, but he felt so unbelievably elated and happy that it was tempting to order a second vodka and a second slice of cake …

He was on his third vodka and his third slice when Dmitri came into the buffet with a telegram. 'I just took this down,' said Dmitri, whose habitually red face, Ivan noticed, looked suddenly pale. 'It's from your wife.'

Ivan Ozolin reached up and took the telegram and read: *Women, too, have the right to escape. I am leaving you, Ivan Andreyevich. I hope to start a flower shop in Tula. Please do not follow me.* Signed: *Your unhappy wife, Anna Borisovna Ozolina.*

Ivan re-read this message several times, while Dmitri stood by him, with his arms hanging limply by his sides.

'What do you make of it?' said Dmitri at last.

'Well,' said Ivan, 'she was always fond of flowers, especially violets.'

'But why would she leave you, Ivan?'

'Because she's tired of my jokes. I don't blame her at all.'

Dmitri sat down. He yawned. He said in a melancholy voice that History had come to them and taken up residence and was now leaving again. He asked Ivan what he planned to do once they found themselves quite alone once more.

Ivan thought about this question for a long time and then he said, 'The woods can look very beautiful at this time of year. I thought I might go mushroom picking.'

The Nettle Pit

JONATHAN COE was born in Birmingham in 1961. His novels include *The Rotters' Club, The Accidental Woman, A Touch of Love, The House of Sleep* and *What a Carve Up!*, which won the 1995 John Llewellyn Rhys Prize and the French Prix du Meilleur Livre Étranger. His latest novel is *The Rain Before it Falls* (2007).

'CHEATING IS AN INTERESTING CONCEPT, don't you think?' said Chris.

'How do you mean?' said Max.

Caroline stood against the kitchen sink and watched the two men talking. Even from this seemingly insignificant exchange, she felt that she could detect a world of difference between them. Chris was a skilled and attractive conversationalist: however small the subject, he would approach it enquiringly, quizzically, endeavouring always to penetrate to the truth and confident that he would get there. Max was perpetually nervous and uncertain – nervous even now, in conversation with the man who was (or so he liked to tell everyone, including himself) his oldest and closest friend. It made her wonder – not for the first time on this holiday – exactly why the fondness between these two men had endured for so long.

'What I mean is, as adults, we don't talk about cheating much, do we?'

'You can cheat on your wife,' said Max, perhaps a touch too wistfully.

'That's the obvious exception,' Chris conceded. 'But otherwise – the concept seems to disappear, doesn't it, some time around teenagerhood? I mean, in football, you talk of players fouling each other, but not cheating. Athletes take performance-enhancing drugs but when it's reported on the news the newsreader doesn't say that so and so's been caught *cheating*. And yet, for little kids, it's an incredibly important concept.'

'Look, I'm sorry—' Max began.

'No, I'm not talking about today,' said Chris. 'Forget about it. It's no big deal.'

Earlier that afternoon Max's daughter Lucy had been involved in a fierce and tearful argument with Chris's youngest, Sara, over alleged cheating during a game of French cricket. They had been playing on the huge expanse of lawn at the front of the house and their screams of reprimand and denial had been heard all over the farm, bringing members of both families running from every direction. The two girls had not spoken to each other since. Even now they were sitting at opposite ends of the farmhouse, one of them frowning over her Nintendo DS, the other flicking through the TV

THE NETTLE PIT

channels, struggling to find anything acceptable to watch on
Irish television.

Chris continued: 'Is Lucy curious about money yet?'

'Not really. We give her a pound every week. She puts it
in a piggy bank.'

'Yes, but does she ever ask you where the money comes
from in the first place? How banks work, and that sort of
thing.'

'She's only seven,' said Max.

'Mm. Well, Joe's getting pretty interested in all that stuff.
He was asking me for a crash course in economics today.'

Yes, he *would* be, Max thought. At the age of eight and
a half, Joe was already starting to manifest his father's om-
nivorous, bright-eyed curiosity, while Lucy, only one year
younger, seemed content to exist in a world of her own,
composed almost entirely of fantasy elements: a world of
dolls and pixies, kittens and hamsters, cuddly toys and benign enchantments. He was trying not to worry about it too
much, or to feel resentment.

'So I told him a little bit about investment banking. You
know, just the basics. I told him that these days, when you
said that someone was a banker, it doesn't mean that he
sits behind a counter and cashes cheques for customers all
day. I told him that a real banker never comes into contact
with money at all. I told him that most of the money in the

47

world nowadays doesn't exist in any tangible form anyway, not even as bits of paper with promises written on them. So he said to me, "But what does a banker *do*, Dad?" So I explained that a lot of modern banking is based on physics. That's where the concept of leverage comes from. And then of course he asked me what leverage was. So I told him that … Well, you can probably imagine what I told him.'

Max nodded, even though he couldn't, in fact, imagine what Chris would have told him. Caroline, who knew her husband well (too well) after all this time, saw the nod and recognised it for the bluff that it was. The little private smile she offered to the kitchen floor was tinged with sadness.

'I told him that a lot of modern banking consists of borrowing money – money that isn't your own – and finding somewhere to reinvest it at a higher rate of return than you're giving to the person you're borrowing it from. And when I told him that, Joe thought about it for a while, and said this very interesting thing: "So bankers," he said, "are really just people who make a lot of money by cheating".'

Max smiled appraisingly. 'Not a bad definition.'

'It isn't, is it? Because it brings a different moral perspective to bear on things. A child's perspective. What the banking community does isn't *illegal* – at least, most of the time. But it does stick in people's throats, and that's why.

At the back of our minds we still have unspoken rules about what's fair and what isn't. And what they do isn't *fair*. It's what children would call cheating.'

Max was still thinking about this conversation later that night, when he and Caroline were lying in bed together, up in the attic bedroom, both on the point of falling asleep.

'I didn't think Chris would have gone for all that "out of the mouths of babes" stuff,' he said. 'Bit too cute for him, I would have thought.'

'Maybe,' said Caroline, non-commitally.

Max waited for her to say more, but there was only silence between them; part of a larger, magical near-silence which hung over the whole of this coastline. If he listened closely, he could just about hear the noise of waves breaking gently on the strand, about half a mile away.

'Close, aren't they?' he prompted.

'Who?' Caroline murmured through her encroaching cloud of sleep.

'Chris and Joe. They spend a lot of time together.'

'Mmm. Well, I suppose that's what fathers and sons do.'

She rolled over slowly and lay flat on her back. Max knew this meant that she was almost asleep now, and conversation was over. He reached out and took her hand. He held on to her hand and looked up at the restless clouds through the bedroom skylight until he heard her breathing become slower and more regular. When she was fully asleep, he gently let go and turned away from her. They had not made love since Lucy was conceived, almost eight years ago.

When they prepared for their walk the next morning, the skies were grey and the estuary tide was low.

The two wives would be staying behind to prepare lunch. Pointedly sporting a plastic apron as her badge of domestic drudgery, Caroline came out onto the lawn to wave the party off, but before they all struck off through the fields and down the path towards the water's edge, Lucy took her parents to one side.

'Come and see this,' she said.

She clasped Max's hand and led him across the wide expanse of lawn towards the hedgerow which marked the boundary of the farmland. Out of the hedge grew a young yew tree, with a single, gnarled branch stretching out back towards the lawn. A piece of knotted rope hung from the branch and, underneath it, the earth had been scooped out to form a deep basin, now choked and brimming with a dense thicket of stinging nettles.

'Wow,' said Max. 'That looks nasty.'

'If you fell in there,' said Lucy, 'would you have to be taken to hospital?'

'Probably not,' said Max. 'But it would really hurt.'

Caroline said: 'Not a very good place to put a rope, really. I don't think you'd better do any swinging on that.'

'But that's our game,' said a boy's breathless voice behind them.

They turned round to see that Joe had run over to join them. His father was following.

'What game would that be?' Caroline asked.

'It's a dare game,' Lucy explained. 'You have to get on the rope and then the others push you and then you have to swing across, like, ten times.'

'I see,' said Chris, in a tone of resigned understanding. 'Somehow this sounds like one of your ideas, Joe.'

'It was, but everybody wants to do it,' his son insisted.

'Well, I don't think you'd better.'

'What would you do', Caroline asked, 'if one of you fell in there? The stinging would be terrible. It would be all over your body.'

'That's the point of the game,' said Joe, with the triumph of one stating the obvious.

'There are lots of dock leaves,' said Lucy. 'So if you fell in you could make yourself better.'

'Five words,' said Caroline. 'No, no, no, no, no.'

Joe let out a sigh of resignation and turned away. But he was not given to brooding on life's disappointments, and his enquiring mind was never at rest for long. As they headed down towards the estuary path, Caroline could hear him asking his father why it was that dock leaves always grew in proximity to stinging nettles, and she could hear his father replying – as always – with a concise, informed explanation. Her eyes followed them as their figures receded, and as Joe's two sisters ran and caught up with them: the bodies of father and son, so alike already in shape and bearing despite the years between them, and the eager, thronging daughters – the three children clustered around their father, drawn together into an inseparable group by blood and mutual affection and above all their unflinching regard for him. And she watched Max and Lucy following them down the same path: hand in hand, yes, but somehow sundered – some force intervening, holding them apart – and sundered in a way that she herself recognised, from personal experience. For an instant, in the odd paradox of their closeness and separation, she saw an emblem of her own relationship with Max. A shaft of keen, indefinable regret pierced her.

Now she could hear the two of them talking as they walked away.

'So why *do* dock leaves always grow next to stinging nettles?' Lucy was asking.

'Well,' Max answered. 'Nature is very clever ...'

But whether he managed to tell her any more than that she couldn't say, their voices being carried off by the sea breeze.

How did he do it, Max found himself wondering on that walk. Just how did Chris get to be so bloody knowledgeable?

He could have understood it if he was just talking about things which fell within his own area of academic expertise. But it wasn't only that. The fact was that he knew everything. Not in an offensive, I'm-cleverer-than-you sort of way. It was merely that he had been alive for forty-three years and in that time he had taken notice of the world around him, absorbed a lot of information and retained it. But why couldn't Max have done that? Why couldn't he remember the simplest things about physics, biology or geography? How could he have lived for so long in the physical world and not learned anything about its laws and principles? It was embarrassing. It made him realise that he was drifting through life in a dream: a dream from which he would maybe awaken one day (probably in about thirty years' time) only to realise that his time on this earth was almost over, before he had even got the slightest handle on it.

Max looked up from these gloomy reflections as he felt Lucy's hand slip out from his grasp, and saw her run away to catch up with Chris and his three children. The genial, ram-shackle, ivy-covered outline of Ballycarberry Castle rose up before them, and she was running towards the point where the river curved, where it was sometimes possible to cross at low tide. Chris was explaining to Joe and his daughters about the tides and the gravitational pull of the moon, a subject (like so many others) of which Max had never achieved anything approaching mastery. He began to half-listen, but then started to feel self-conscious and, by way of distraction, picked up a flat stone, which he attempted to skim across the river's surface. It sank after a couple of bounces. Turning to catch up with the others, he found that Chris had now gathered all four of the children around him beside an ex-posed cross-section of the river bank. Even Lucy seemed to be paying attention.

'Now, when a great chunk of the earth is exposed like this,' Chris was saying, 'the brilliant thing is that it tells you all sorts of stuff about the history of the area. Can anyone remember what these different layers of soil are called?'

'Horizons!' said Joe, keenly.

'That's right. They're called soil horizons. Now, normally the top layer – this thin, dark layer here – is known as the 'O' horizon, but this one would be classified as a 'P' horizon, because this part of the countryside is so watery. Do you know what 'P' stands for – something that you find a lot in Ireland?'

'Peat?'

'Peat, exactly! Then we have the topsoil, and the subsoil. Notice how the different horizons get lighter and lighter as you get further down. Even here, though, the subsoil is still quite dark. That's because Ireland has a very rainy climate and rain is very effective in breaking down rock to form soil, and also in distributing nutrients through the soil. But the soil here is also quite sandy, because we're at the mouth of an estuary.'

'What is an estuary, Dad?'

'An estuary is any coastal area where fresh water from rivers and streams mixes with salt water from the ocean. So, estuaries form the boundaries between terrestrial systems and marine systems. They tend to have very rich soil because it's full of decaying plants and animals. Look here in the subsoil, for instance ...'

Oh, it was impressive stuff, Max had to admit. But then, you would expect Chris to know about soil. He had been teaching geology at university level for twenty years, and now he was a senior lecturer. Max wondered if his daughter realised this. Probably not. She was starting to stare at him with the same starry-eyed adoration as his own children.

Soon Chris, his daughters and Joe moved on, chatting away happily, making for the three stone steps which had been cut roughly into the wall, allowing people to climb up onto the walkway and thence along the grassy path to the castle itself. Lucy, meanwhile, lingered uncertainly. She took her father's hand again and looked up into his eyes. It wasn't at all clear that she had understood the finer points of that little lecture, but she had definitely understood something: she had understood the bonds of faith and admiration that connected Chris's children to their father; she had understood the cheerful reverence with which they had listened to him. She had understood all of this, and Max knew, now, that she was wondering why the same feelings did not bind her to her own father. Or, rather, she was now groping for those feelings, with a kind of forlorn hope. She wanted to be talked to in that way. She wanted her father to explain the world to her, with the same confidence and authority that Chris beamed out to his children with every word. As they, too, began to walk on, she looked around her, and Max knew that she was taking in her surroundings with a new kind of curiosity; knew that she was going to have questions of her own to ask him, soon, and that he would be expected to have the answers.

It happened sooner than he had been anticipating.

'Daddy,' she began, innocently enough.

'Mmm?' said Max, stiffening himself for the impending curve ball.

'Daddy, why is the grass green?'

Max laughed, as though this was the simplest and most innocuous question in the world; opened his mouth to allow the answer to fall almost carelessly from his lips; then stopped, as he realised that he didn't have the faintest idea what to say.

Why is the grass green? What kind of question was that? It just *was* green. Everybody knew that. It was one of those things you took for granted. Had anybody ever explained to *him* why the grass was green? At school, maybe? What would that have come under – biology, geography? That was ages ago. Of course Chris would know, yes. He would know that it was something to do with ... was it chromo-something, some word like that? Didn't *chromo* mean *colour* in Greek, or Latin? Chromosomes – was it something to do with chromosomes? Or that other thing that sunlight did to plants ... photo ... photo ... photosynthesis. Was that what made things go green ...?

He glanced down at Lucy. She was looking up at him patiently, trustingly. She seemed very young, for a moment, younger even than her seven years.

It was no use. Silence would be the worst response of all. He was going to have to tell her *something*.

'Well …' he began. 'Well, every night, the fairies come out, with their little paintbrushes and their pots of green paint …'

God, he hated himself sometimes.

Caroline and Miranda had finished preparing lunch some time ago, and were relaxing at the kitchen table, a bottle of red wine sitting between them, already half-emptied.

'You see,' Caroline was saying, 'the trouble with Max is …'

But there lay the problem. What *was* the trouble with Max? And even if she knew, should she really be confiding it in this woman, the wife of her husband's best friend, a woman she barely knew? (Although she was already getting to know – and like – her pretty well on this holiday.) Wouldn't that in itself be a kind of betrayal?

She sighed, giving up – as usual – the struggle to put her finger on it. 'I don't know … He just doesn't seem very happy, that's all. There's something about his life … about himself … Something that he doesn't like.'

'He's very quiet,' Miranda conceded. 'But I assumed he was always like that.'

'He's always been quiet,' said Caroline. 'But it's been getting worse lately. Sometimes I can't seem to get a word out of him. I suppose he talks all day at work.' Changing tack, she said: 'I wonder what he and Chris have in common. They're such different people, and yet they've been friends for so long. Ever since school.'

'Well, that counts for a lot in itself, doesn't it? Shared history, and so on.' Miranda could sense something bearing down upon Caroline, some weight of apprehension. 'Lots of couples go through difficult times,' she said. 'And Lucy seems very close to her father.'

'You think so?' Caroline shook her head. 'They *want* to be close. But they don't know how to do it. *He* doesn't know how to do it.' Attempting to drain off her wine glass, but finding it empty, she said: 'What Lucy would really like is a brother or sister. Your Joe looks in seventh heaven, with a big sister and a little sister to play with. It's so great, seeing the three of them like that. How families should be …'

'It's not too late, is it?'

Caroline smiled. 'I'm not too old, if that's what you mean. But it's probably too late in other ways.' She reached for the bottle, refilled their glasses, and took what was more than a sip. 'Ah well. *Would've, should've, could've*. The most painful words in the language.'

How much further this conversation would have progressed, how much more dangerously confiding Caroline might have become, they would never know. At that moment the back door of the farmhouse was flung open. They could hear the distressed voices of children and adults from the garden, and now Chris rushed purposefully into the kitchen, looking harassed and short of breath.

'Quick,' he said. 'Where's the first aid box?'

Miranda jumped to her feet.

'What's happened? Who's hurt?'

'It's Joe, mainly. Lucy a bit, as well. Baking soda – that's what we need. Do we have any baking soda?'

'But what *happened*?'

Without waiting to hear the answer, Caroline ran outside onto the lawn, where a scene of chaos was awaiting her. Joe lay stretched out on the grass, motionless; at first she thought that he was unconscious. Max was kneeling beside him, a hand laid tenderly on his brow. Lucy came running to meet her mother, and flung herself at her, clasping her fiercely with bare arms which, she could not help noticing, were mottled and livid with angry crimson blotches.

'What have you done to yourself, love? What happened?'

'It was the nettle game,' Lucy told her, between sobs. 'The dare. We came back from the castle and then started playing it and Daddy was pushing Joe on the rope. He was swinging really hard and then he fell off and landed right in the middle of the pit. I climbed in and tried to help him out.'

'That was brave of you.'

'It really, really hurts.'

'I bet it does. Don't worry. Chris and Miranda will be out here, any second now. They're finding some stuff to put on it.'

'What about Joe? He was wearing shorts and everything. His legs ...'

Caroline turned to look at the figures of Joe, stretched out on the lawn, and her husband at his side. In just a few seconds Joe's father and mother would have reached their son, tending to him, ministering to his needs. But in years to come, it would not be those next few minutes' confusion and frantic activity that Caroline would remember. It would be this one moment of stillness: the tableau (as she would always recall it) she saw laid out before her as she turned. The prostrate body of Joe, who had indeed passed out, either with the shock or with the pain, lying so still, and so reposeful, that one might even imagine him to have died. And kneeling beside him – crying, too, unless Caroline was mistaken – her husband, fixated by the pain and distress not of his own daughter, but of another man's child. And the strange thing about it was that, after watching Max so closely, and with so much bewilderment, during the last few days, after tormenting herself with the riddle of his unhappiness, his maladjustment, his sense of being for ever ill at ease in the world, at that moment she saw him – or imagined that she saw him – in an attitude that for once

JONATHAN COE

suited him, and made perfect sense: she saw him as a man surrendering to a feeling that must have come so naturally, with such a healing inevitability, that it might almost have - felt like a release; a man in mourning over the death of the son he had always wanted.

Boys in Cars

MARTI LEIMBACH is the author of several novels, including the international bestseller *Dying Young*, which was made into a film starring Julia Roberts, and the acclaimed *Daniel Isn't Talking* (2007), inspired by the story of her autistic child. Her latest book, *The Man from Saigon*, a love story between news reporters during the Vietnam war, will be published in 2009. Born in Washington DC, she moved to England in 1990; she lives in Berkshire with her husband and two children.

WE THINK WE KNOW HIM because we know his label, and this informs all our thoughts. He is meant to be aloof, preferring his own company to that of his classmates, for example. But when the birthday invitation arrives, he presents it to me in the envelope with his name, Alex, in another mother's florid script, and I think I see him smile.

'You've got mail,' he says in a perfect imitation of our computer.

'Go on, open it,' I tell him.

'You could already be our grand prize winner!'

Television speak. He can sing jingles, reel off 0800 numbers, imitate beer commercials, and tell me with perfect commercial inflection that past performance is not a reliable indicator of future performance. So I am unsure if it is the birthday invitation that intrigues him or the opportunity it affords to parrot yet another slogan. Just as I have this thought, he seems to change. Instead of smiling, he tenses, then cranes his neck. He's about to run off but I loop my elbow through his so he cannot escape. 'See what's inside!' I urge.

'This is for me,' he says, and now it is his own voice, Alex's voice, telling me to mind my business.

'All right, but wouldn't it be a good idea to see what is inside?'

He seems perplexed, turning the envelope over several times. When finally he uncovers the invitation, he lifts it gently by the corners as though handling a film negative. On it is the name of the birthday boy, a time and date. There is also a location, a farm park, and I can tell exactly the moment Alex realises that this party will take place among donkeys and ducks, sheep and miniature ponies, none of which he can stand. He looks at the invitation as though it is the foul excretion of one such animal, then places it on the bulletin board next to his rail schedule.

'Three o'clock is 15:00,' he says. 'It is when the Great Western train leaves Reading station from Platform 5. I cannot go to this party.'

'Fifteen-oh-oh' is how he says it. He goes to school at eight-three-oh. His bedtime is twenty-one-oh-oh.

I point out that there will be a lot of children from his class there and that he will miss out on the fun.

'Cows smell,' he says.

'But they make milk. Don't you want to try to milk a cow? Or feed the chickens?' I am duty-bound to bring a tide

66

of enthusiasm, hoping some of it will rub off, but frankly it never does. Alex twirls his school tie, a knotted bit of synthetic blue on an elastic cord. Twisting the tie around his finger, he rocks his weight from one foot to another, staring at the invitation, and then touching it with his nose.

'No,' he says.

'What if you come at the end, maybe just for some cake and juice?'

'I think I would rather play on the computer,' he says. This is true, of course. And the fact that it is true now, and that it is almost certainly going to be true at three o'clock on a Saturday two weeks from now, is part of what is wrong.

'But this is the first birthday party you've had all year.' My voice is a careful mixture of gentleness and persuasion. What I am saying is that he will go.

He rocks a little harder, glances at me, then at the invitation. He untacks his rail schedule, his favourite possession aside from his computer, and re-tacks it so that it covers the whole of the invitation, although there is a little corner where the 'Y' from the word 'party' can still be read.

Now he looks at me, scanning my face. 'You don't see that,' he says.

Our house is a brick box in a row of brick boxes. The front door is a stained mahogany colour, but otherwise it is as close to feature-free as you can get while still having windows. When I first saw the house with Richard, my architect husband – now my ex-husband – he said, 'It is like a dentist's office, without magazines.'

'Yes,' I said, holding up a finger, 'but that isn't necessarily a bad thing.' It was all we could afford. I saw no reason to disparage it. 'We have nice furniture. That will make a difference. And we'll play Monteverdi's Vespers in the mornings. We'll create – you know – atmosphere.'

I smiled. Richard grunted. I didn't know it but already he was falling in love with Carla, a draughtsman at his firm. A draughtswoman. Another woman, anyway.

'I like our old house,' he said. Alex, then three years old, was in the car just outside the front door. I could see him perfectly through the window, strapped into his car seat, silent, with that same studious, slightly worried expression that had taken over every other expression he'd once had.

We'd already received the offer we hoped for on our old house. We needed that money for Alex's intensive speech and language therapy. I was thinking practical. I was thinking Alex. Anyway, I'd already bought the little house, a fact I withheld for a time.

It has been so many years since Alex learned to speak that

now I take it for granted. Sometimes his language arrives in disordered fragments – verbs at the end of a sentence as though he is translating from German, or the answer 'yes' to every question, like a new immigrant who finds the native tongue hard to decipher but wants to please.

Tonight, at dinner, Alex is very clear. First, he states that he does not eat green things, as I ought to know, and second that he does not eat fruit. He tells me this while folding his homework in half, then quarters, then eighths, then sixteenths. All over the house are pieces of paper that he has folded and then unfolded in various fashions. He likes patterns of diamonds and squares and triangles. For years, I have had to iron his homework each morning before school.

'Alex, there is no fruit on your plate,' I tell him now.

He holds up a biscuit, one of the homemade ones I have sweetened with dates and honey.

He says, 'Fruit is like an excretion from earth. I can't eat it.'

I shrug my shoulders. 'Where do you see fruit?'

'Hidden.'

'I don't see it.'

'Something is here,' he says. 'I don't know. But it is from a tree.'

He returns to his homework page, which he unfolds, showing an elaborate pattern of diamonds and parallel lines.

I smile at his creation because he is so proud. He thinks he has made something beautiful, though I know the teacher will be less impressed.

'So let me get this right,' I say. 'Nothing green and nothing from a tree.'

He nods, then places the biscuit onto the plate and covers the plate with his napkin.

I say, 'Oranges are from trees.'

This makes him cross. He loves orange juice. He looks at his glass, perhaps deciding whether he can permit himself to drink juice now that this fact about the orange has been brought to his attention.

'No bits,' he tells me sternly. 'Smooth style only. Tropicana only.'

'Okay, but even Tropicana is made from oranges, which are a fruit, and come from trees,' I say. I want him to understand that, despite how much he denies it, he is as reliant on the facts of nature as the rest of us.

'Just the juice, not the bits. None of these.' He pushes the plate of biscuits, shrouded in their napkin, to the centre of the table. Years ago he'd have hurled them to the floor, but those days are over. We have this other thing – his rigid ideas, what would be obstinacy in another child – but not destruction.

'What do you eat when you visit Daddy?' I ask him.

'Nothing,' he says. Then, after a moment, he says, 'Meat.'

Richard now lives in a Victorian flat outside Ealing. It has huge windows and a vaulted ceiling and sealed wooden floors; everything solid, no aluminium. He was the third casualty after the house, and after Alex, himself, who changed at about twenty months, the first symptom being that he stopped smiling.

Two years ago, when Alex was six, I took him to Richard's flat for their first weekend together. He walked the perimeter of the place, his ear cocked as though listening to the waves of traffic below, then threw himself onto the floor, his fists clenched, his face screwed in concentrated agony, screaming in protest as though some invisible force were holding him down.

'But you will have a great time with Daddy!' I said, trying to reassure him. His shirt rode up his middle, his shoes hammered the varnished floor and, when I tried to stop him kicking, he caught my thumb and bit it. I heard a little gasp, then realised it was my own. A phone rang and Richard's voice came on, announcing that Carla and he were not at home.

'AHHHH!' Alex yelled. I dropped my head, closed my eyes, trying to absorb this moment like so many others, feeling it enter me, unlock my heart, tattoo a little mark right there.

'He's going to take you to see rockets at the Science Museum. And stars at the Planetarium!' I promised. The caller began to leave an elaborate message for Carla, something about where the wine bar was located and what time they would all meet. Meanwhile, Alex looked like he'd been put on a stretching rack, his legs tensed, toes pointing, his back arched so that his stomach rose like a table in front of me. 'It's – not –' He couldn't quite get his words out. But he had words – that was the point. The sale of our old house bought us his ability to speak. After hours and hours of therapy; I'd say it was a bargain.

'It's – not – !'

'It's not what, Alex?' I said gently.

But he cannot talk when he is upset (this is still the case). He gave up, pounding the floor, pressing his eyes with his fingers, groaning. Richard stood over us, a giant, angry scarecrow. 'What is the matter?' he asked Alex, a little sharply.

'It's – not – square!' Alex yelled. And then I realised that it wasn't the thought of being in a new place that bothered him, or the thought of being with his father for the weekend, or having Carla there instead of me. It was that the walls were not true in the flat. The shape was not geometric, being neither rectangular nor square.

'Okay, okay, it's not square, but …' I thought for a moment. 'It's still a quadrilateral,' I said.

Richard turned and went to the window. 'Let him cry,' he said.

I looked up. 'He's only six.'

'If he's old enough to know what is square, he's old enough to stop crying.'

This kind of logic had been the wrecking ball of our marriage.

What I learned that day was important. Not about my ex-husband being a jerk – I already knew that. Carla could have him. Being an architect herself, maybe she could remodel him into something more spacious, more inviting. What I learned was the importance of changing my house around, not letting Alex get too stuck on 'sameness'. I can't do anything about the walls, which are all perfectly aligned, but I can alter curtains so that they don't hang exactly right, swap around colours and furniture. Make a bedroom into a study, the living room into a bedroom, then switch it back again.

Alex hates this. But I notice that he accepts such changes now with resignation. Tonight, after a dinner during which he eats nothing green and nothing from a tree unless it is orange juice, he climbs the steps to his bedroom. There the computer waits for him, his faithful companion, purring like a cat.

The first thing he sees is that I have painted his door.

'It's green!' he calls down. 'It should be white!'

'It's still a door,' I say in a chipper sort of way.

'And there is a tree on it!'

'Yes, an oak,' I tell him. 'I painted some acorns at the bottom.'

Inside his room is a rug with one corner cut out of it – another part of my cunning plan to combat inflexibility. But I noticed this morning when I was putting away clothes that he had filled in the missing corner with permanent marker, which he drew across the floor.

I deserved it, I suppose. But the door is a bushy green English oak now and I can hear his sigh from all the way down here.

'Stupid door!' he says. 'Stupid, stupid, stupid!'

The week before the birthday party, I uncover the invitation from its place behind the railway schedule, securing it with strong tacks at each of its corners. The next day I check to see whether he has hidden it again, but it is still in full view. It is there the day after that. And the next.

'This is a great invitation,' I tell him.

'It has balloons,' he says, then sucks his lips so that his mouth seems to disappear.

'You'll be nine soon, too,' I say, inserting a measure of intrigue into my voice, like his turning nine is a splendid new thing. 'Maybe you'll have a party.'

'I like eight,' he tells me.

But the invitation remains. I am hoping that the fact he allows it to remain means he has brought the birthday party into his horizon, expecting it, maybe half looking forward to it. I think the party excites him and frightens him. He looks at the invitation, wringing his hands like a racetrack punter, occasionally standing for many minutes with it inches from his nose. Throughout the day he checks the rail schedule and then glances at the clock, calculating perhaps the number of minutes it will take before the Bedwyn train stops at Newbury, our local station, or how many London trains are scheduled that hour. Then he looks at the invitation. I see his eyes move with the words he reads. I see him smile and then put his hand over his mouth.

'There will be cake,' he says to no one in particular.

The cuckoo clock was always his favourite toy. It always cuckooed, or whatever you call it, exactly on the hour.

Film times, listed in bulleted lights across a black screen, held him for ages. He danced beneath them, memorising the times for any number of films he had no interest in seeing, preferring always to watch videos.

A single video will wear out after about 150 viewings; this I have learned.

The first song on the album must be the first song you listen to. The last song on the album must be the last song you listen to. When I program the CD player for random selection, he says, 'Uh-oh,' then shakes his head and reprograms it.

'That's not right,' he says, like he's talking about ethics. About truth. 'That's not right,' he says, when I mix Tomy trains with a Bob the Builder machine.

It is as though he wishes for more order. The things he loves – computer games, music playlists, the building of robots – all function within a closed, static system.

But I am not a static system. When I speak, I go off on tangents, or change my mind, or change the subject, or pause too long. I might sneeze, cough. My facial gestures, my gaze and movements, are too random for Alex. He looks away.

'Talk to me,' I beg him, speaking to the side of his neck.

'It's good to talk,' he says, Vodafone-style.

In the car, on the way to school, I try to hook him into con-versation. 'Look, an alien from outer space!' I say, pointing at a cloud. He tells me, frankly, that it is only a seagull. 'But the alien was riding the seagull!' I say, to which he announces that I am annoying him. 'I like to annoy people,' I tease. 'If you want me to stop, you better call the Silly Police.'

'Silly Police,' he repeats.

'They will stop me,' I assure him.

A few minutes later, I say, 'The alien was riding a seagull with green feathers.'

'Silly Police!' Alex says. 'And there was no seagull.'

I try several other manners of engaging him during the journey. All he wants to do is sit. Finally, somewhat apologetically, he confesses, 'You are confusing me.'

I nod. I tell him, 'I know. But I am confused, too.'

'It is because I am autistic,' he announced once after a prickly meeting with his classroom teacher. Both Richard and I attended the meeting, which was about how Alex was not socialising enough, was not *assimilating*, to use her words.

Richard exploded. 'Who the hell taught him that?!' he shouted as Alex clasped his ears.

'One of the other children at school told him,' I explained. I cleared my throat, looking straight ahead. It hadn't been another child; it was me. Alex sometimes cries silently, sitting in bed, staring ahead as at a film only he can see. A few nights earlier he said, 'I am not like the other boys.' And then those odd, quiet tears. So I told him.

'You can't expect other children to follow your ideas,' I said to Richard. 'If he goes to a mainstream school, kids are going to talk. That's just the way it is.'

'Bloody school,' said Richard.

I sighed. I hated myself for lying. 'It's not such a bad thing that he knows.'

'It is 19:14,' Alex told his father. 'Your train is at 19:31.'

I shouldn't be relieved when Richard leaves, but I always am.

'Shall I walk on my hands?' I ask him, 'Shall I eat with my nose?' I pretend to be a bird, pecking spaghetti from my plate. Alex cannot stand it, of course. 'Stop that,' he says.

I iron his homework and he tells me, 'That's not clothes.'

I brush my hair with a toothbrush and he shakes his head.

'Rule violation?' I tease.

His lips lift in a half-smile. 'I'm calling the Silly Police,' he says.

This is progress.

Most of the time it is a question of intrusion.

'I want to go on the computer,' he says. It's like a sign on the door saying 'No Entry'.

'I want to go on the Alex,' I tell him.

'You can't go on me,' he says. 'I'm not a machine.'

This is the thing I am counting on. That he knows he is not a machine, and that he is willing – now or someday – to take risks, to enter into the complex, broadband style of communication the rest of us have. That he will not want to remain always within the safety of the predictable – videos, timetables, computer games, Lego instructions – but will seek out the erratic, shifting world of social exchange. Seek it out, not be pushed into it.

'I'm not going to the birthday party,' he tells me. 'I don't like mammals.'

For the birthday party he has a new pair of combat trousers I picked up at Marks and Spencer's. He has chosen a shirt he has used a clothing marker on, drawing the exact places on the shirt beneath which you would find his inner organs. He thinks it is cool, this shirt, but I doubt the other children will agree.

He combs his hair straight down with a damp comb, brushes his teeth, smiles into the mirror and then lets his smile fall.

'What is our departure time?' he says.

'Fourteen-four-oh,' I tell him.

The invitation has been folded so tightly that the patterns seem infinite, like those of a crystal. He sits in the car with his gleaming hair, his clear brown eyes. Every so often he makes an odd grimacing smile that looks neither natural nor joyful.

'Birthday parties are boring,' he says. He has undoubtedly heard this said by someone in his class about maths or train times. His tone and his expression as he says it seem as though they come from someone else, another child, not Alex.

On the way to the birthday party I tell him that I can stay with him or I can go – it's up to him.

He says nothing; I don't even know if he has heard me. He licks his lips over and over. Below his lower lip is a chafed area the shape of a crescent moon.

'I can chat with the other mothers,' I say.

He closes his eyes, then shudders, licks his lips again. I would ask him to stop but I know he can't help it. He is doing his best, I tell myself. He is trying.

'You're doing great,' I tell him.

Then he starts to cry. His tears are silent, falling one at a time in a steady stream down his cheeks.

'Oh sweetheart,' I say, searching the kerb for a place to pull over, feeling that same unlocking that I have become so familiar with. I am marked like a dartboard. As I pull to the side of the road, Alex opens his mouth to speak, but all that comes out is a single, long moan.

He was not always like this. In our old house, the one Richard mourned so much, he chased me across the cherry wood floor, laughing as I hid from him, springing out from behind doors to surprise me. He made baby sounds and touched my lips as I imitated back to him his mysterious cooings. We have photographs of him dancing with a stuffed bear, turning sand with a shovel, testing his skill with a tricycle. And we have the other photographs, too, in which his eyes seem heavy, his gaze vacant, his expression dulled. Autism has taken from us and we are not the same. Like people in a country that has suffered a long and brutal war, we have lived under its siege, uncertain of our future, facing daily the great and menacing spectre before us as though with one eye.

'I'm tired,' Richard said when I called him about the party. 'I can't have him this weekend. Carla wants to go away.'

Richard sounded worse than tired. He sounded depressed. Or drunk, or perhaps a mixture of the two. Sometimes I remind myself that this is hard: for me, for him, for Alex.

'That's okay; he has a birthday party anyway. I'm happy for him to stay home – I mean, with me.'

'A birthday party? He'll hate that.'

'It will be fine,' I said. Richard coughed, then laughed unpleasantly. He said Alex wouldn't make it through a party. And that I was crazy.

'Of course he'll make it through,' I said, trying to sound confident, trying to sound like I know my son.

'Don't call me all tearful when it goes to shit,' he said.

'I won't call you.'

In the car I stroke Alex's hair. I tell him it's just a party. We don't have to go. On his lap is a present he has chosen for the birthday boy, a train that you can take apart and put together again with a plastic screwdriver. It is exactly the sort of thing Alex loves and he has chosen it for another boy. This is a step forward. Some ridiculous and practical part of me wants to move the present from his lap now, as his tears are making the wrapping soggy. But he clasps it tightly, hanging on as though to a ledge from which he might fall.

'We don't have to go to the party,' I tell him.

'I'm a silly boy,' he says.

'No, not silly. Wonderful. A wonderful boy.'

'Silly, useless boy!' he says. And still the tears, one after the other, following the same track.

What I must remind myself of now – what I must tell

myself – is that it is good that Alex wants to share how he feels. This moment, however painful, signifies a change. Because it is all the things he is not doing that matter. He is *not* having a tantrum. He is not hitting his head against the dashboard, kicking his legs out straight, biting his own hand. What he is doing is so normal. He is telling me how he feels and with that he is showing an expectation, I think, this somehow communicating his feelings will make it better. Surely we are getting now to the real problem, the very core of the autism that holds him back, that hurts him.

'Right now, in other cars, are boys like you,' I tell him. I have no idea where this is going, but I keep talking. 'They are nervous that nobody will like them. That at the party they will be afraid ... of the animals or the noise or ... or that there will be too many colours—'

'And the balloons might pop!' he cries.

'Exactly,' I agree. 'The balloons might pop. They are concerned about that.'

'And that's a horrid noise!' he says. 'And the children running in all directions!'

I nod. 'Yes,' I say. I take his hand and he squeezes my fingers; I am amazed by how hard.

'They might be worried,' he says, shaking. There is a heat rising from him; he's on fire with worry, it seems. How do I stop this? How do I make him happy again? Do I return him to his computer? Do I take him to the railway station and let him watch the trains?

'Yes, they might be worried,' I say. With emphasis I add: 'But they don't have to go.'

Now he moans as though in terrible pain. 'Yes they do!' he says. The T-shirt on which he has marked his pancreas and large intestines, his stomach and heart, is getting wet. All the ribs are beginning to blur; both his lungs. 'Yes they dooooo!'

'Okay, but they don't have to go *today*,' I tell him.

For a long while we are like this. He cries; I hold his hand. His carefully combed hair stands up straight with the heat of his body. Cars pass us, some with families aboard. None of them know why we are pulled over at the bus stop. Not even this bus, angling behind us, has any clue why we are here.

The windows are steamed up. Alex's crying slows, now stops, but the windows shed drops of moisture in long, slow streams.

'Are you okay?' I ask him.

He shakes his head sadly, his mouth turned down.

'Let's go home,' I say, and turn the ignition.

'No,' he says.

I don't think we should stay here much longer – the bus driver wasn't too pleased with my blocking him – and there's no way we can go to the party now. Richard was right. Mrs Whatsit, his teacher, was right.

'Are we late?' Alex asks. 'Is it 15:00 yet?'

It is already ten past three, but Alex doesn't look at the clock, perhaps because he doesn't really want to know. He hates to be late to anything. He might find it impossible to go at all if he knows he would be late. 'Not yet,' I tell him.

'Go now,' he says. 'To the party.' He sniffs, rubs his eyes with his shirt, the one with the parts of the body, the one he thinks is cool. When I hesitate he looks at me, his mouth opening. What he needs is for me to tell him just one more time that he can do this. That he can manage a birthday party just as he has managed so many things. So I do my best to smile as I put the car into gear.

'Somebody has to be a friend to those boys,' I tell him. 'Those other boys in cars right now.'

'I will be their friend,' he says. He sets his jaw, looking ahead.

This is the moment I will remember as the turning point, a moment that begins with that change in his expression. He glances at me, then reaches over and takes the invitation from my lap. I had forgotten it was there, so when he plucks it from my lap, it is as though he produces it from thin air. On it are directions that he reads to me now, clearly and slowly and in the manner of a young man reading directions to a driver, who is his companion – a friend, a girlfriend, a wife perhaps. I can see it now. One day he will have a wife. And he will be able to go to such a thing as a party. He will have choices and this, if nothing else, makes him no different than other people. The future is not nearly so bleak as it seemed even five minutes ago. It will be all right, after all. He is making a choice. This is a fact, as palpable as the ledge of his kneecap beneath my palm, or the startling sound of seagulls descending low in the sky, appearing out of nowhere like a cloud, welcoming us forward with their caws.

Lucky We
Live Now

KATE ATKINSON was born in York in 1951 and studied English Literature at Dundee University, where she later taught. She currently lives in Edinburgh. Her first novel, *Behind the Scenes at the Museum*, won the Whitbread Book of the Year and she has been a critically acclaimed, international bestselling author ever since. Her latest novels – *Case Histories, One Good Turn* and *When Will There Be Good News?* – all feature former police inspector Jackson Brodie.

Annihilating all that's made
To a green thought in a green shade
from *The Garden* by Andrew Marvell

IT BEGAN WITH THE MOTHS. Genevieve woke up early but in these times of austerity it was too cold to leave a warm bed and too dark to do much anyway. She wished she had a boyfriend to keep her warm in the bleak midwinter. Her boyfriend walked into the freezing fog one night and never came back. Genevieve liked to think of it as a mysterious disappearance but she knew he was living across town with an actress called Melanie who did throaty voice-overs for public information broadcasts, telling people how to cook with hay boxes and emphasising the importance of sealing up draughty windows.

'The theatre is needed more than ever in times of austerity,' thieving Melanie had declared pompously in an interview that Genevieve listened to on her wind-up radio. Where other celebrities' fame had dimmed and faded, Melanie's star now shone brightly (the 'Voice of Austerity'). She was right, though, people craved entertainment now that there was no more getting and spending. They huddled in theatres, flocking to opera, to pantomimes, to mystery plays – anything that provided government-subsidised spectacle.

Or a dog. A dog would keep her warm at night. You didn't see too many about, now that it was no longer illegal to sell dog meat. The dog shelter had been emptied overnight when the law was rescinded. Any day now, Genevieve expected to hear a purring Melanie on the wind-up radio giving advice on the best way to spit-roast a Labrador.

Genevieve fumbled in the dark for the box of matches that was somewhere on her bedside table. The match flared reluctantly into life and Genevieve lit the stub of a candle. The sight of a naked flame flickering in the dark made her feel strangely hollow inside. She thought fondly of electricity, the way you thought of an old, dead, friend. She was sorry she had taken it for granted and not paid it more attention. The flick of a switch and it had gone.

The candle flame fluttered wildly in a draught from the window that she had not – in rebellious defiance of Melanie's admonition – sealed up. It was at that moment that the moths appeared, an angry mob of them suddenly bursting out of the wardrobe. Genevieve had a brief glimpse of their thick, hairy bodies (a surprisingly lovely colour, like Jersey cream) before the downdraught from a roomful of frantically beating wings extinguished the light. Moths to a flame, she supposed. She would have screamed but she imagined the moths swarming into her mouth and suffocating her, their papery wings stuck in her throat, so instead she slid under the bedcovers and hid there until daylight.

When she finally dared to look out from the sheets, there was no sign of the moths and Genevieve supposed that she must have dreamt them. When she stepped out of bed, however, her feet crunched on something underfoot and she found that the carpet was covered in what looked like hairy, white mints. It took her quite a while to identify them as cocoons – coffin and casket, winding-sheet and swaddling clothes, all rolled into one.

She realised that she was being watched, and experienced an icy, horror-movie chill spill down her spine. Looking cautiously round the room she realised that she hadn't dreamt the moths. They were everywhere – perched on the picture rail, clinging to the mirror frame, folded into the curtains. Hundreds of little, unblinking black-bead eyes observing her. Here and there, tiny antennae twitched. Genevieve spotted the occasional slow-motion beat of a wing as a moth opened and closed itself like a small, fragile book. They seemed to be waiting for something.

'Moths?'
　　'Yes, moths.'
　　'Clothes moths?' her mother asked.
　　'Well, they seem to have eaten all my clothes, although they looked like silk moths.'
　　'They ate all of your clothes?'
　　'No. Just the things made from silk.'
　　'Silk?'
　　'Silk,' Genevieve confirmed.
　　'That's almost like cannibalism,' her mother said thoughtfully.

Clothes were precious, finite things. After all the mills and factories closed, women knitted through the night by candlelight and wished they had listened to their grandmothers who had tried to teach them to darn. The streets were filled with people wearing misshapen knitted garments.

　　There was a fashion for spinning wheels. Some women pricked their fingers on spindles and fell asleep, the yarn spooling their bodies until they were like bobbins. Like cocoons. Clothes maketh the woman.

People bought treadle sewing machines in auctions. In the time of austerity everyone looked as if they had been patched together from rags. 'Handmade is the new high fashion,' Melanie's voice intoned over the airwaves. 'Make jam, not war. Knit someone you love a scarf.' ('Oh, please,' Genevieve's mother said to Genevieve, 'don't.')

'Remember Selfridges?' Genevieve said dreamily to the moths. 'And the Top Shop mothership on Oxford Street? Liberty's. Peter Jones. Harvey Nichols.' The names were like poetry in the mouth, like chocolate on the tongue. Genevieve thought about the layers of department stores, like big cakes filled with lovely things. It used to feel so good to hand over a credit card and get something in return.

Genevieve was a garden designer. She used to design beautiful gardens for a lot of money, but no one wanted expensive, ornamental gardens in the bleak midwinter. Instead they were digging them up and planting cabbages and potatoes in the mud. Genevieve's mother didn't have a garden but, a practical woman, she kept an Eglu in her spare bedroom. People grew vegetables in window boxes and in tubs on balconies. There were pigs in back gardens in the New Town. No ducks on Blackford pond any more; they were all laying eggs in people's bathrooms and cellars.

Genevieve fell asleep to the faint, fairy rustle of moth wings.

KATE ATKINSON

There didn't seem to be any way of getting rid of them. There were no mothballs in the shop, no camphor, no lavender sachets or cedar chests. There were, let's face it, no shops. Things could be worse, her mother said. It could have been hornets.

Next it was goats. A medium-sized flock that must have arrived in the middle of the night because they were already there when Genevieve woke up, grazing on the carpet and nibbling the bedspread. When she looked in her wardrobe all her cashmere had disappeared. She phoned her mother.

'Goats have eaten all my cashmere.'

'They eat anything,' her mother said. 'How many?'

Genevieve counted them. 'Nine.'

'You know it takes four years for one goat to produce enough cashmere for a sweater,' her mother said. 'The very best cashmere comes from the underbelly and the throat. You should get shearing.'

Genevieve tried to imagine shaving a goat's throat. It seemed like an overly poetic act.

'Come to tea,' her mother said. 'I've got an egg.'

The next day her mother arrived with a small, sharp, silver knife in her pocket and slaughtered the goats in Genevieve's back garden, cutting their shorn throats. 'Don't worry,' she said, handing Genevieve a handkerchief for her tears. 'We were giving dominion over them. Every creeping thing that creepeth upon earth and so on. You look like you're wearing an old pair of curtains.'

'I am.'

A cow nudged her awake with its huge wet nose. Only one, thank goodness. Its tragic, brown eyes gazed mournfully at her. Perhaps it knew about Genevieve's mother and her small, sharp, silver knife. Genevieve still felt bad about the goats, even though they had tasted delicious. A flurry of moths flitted around the cow's head, like an animated halo. When she got out of bed Genevieve discovered that all her shoes had disappeared. She wondered if it was like the seven plagues of Egypt. Would there be locusts?

No locusts, just a bee. In the kitchen cupboard the sticky film of honey left at the bottom of the jar had turned into a small frustrated bee. Genevieve was beginning to see a pattern. She took the jar outside and unscrewed the lid. The bee flew away. No one else, she noticed, seemed to be having this problem.

When she came back in the house she found an entire flock of bleating sheep shouldering each other down the stairs. They streamed around her and pushed their way out of the back door into the garden. The cow bellowed in soft surprise at the sight of them. Genevieve was left with no knitwear, no Uggs, no blankets, no carpets.

Reivers took all the beasts in the night before her mother could come over with her small, sharp, silver knife. The smell of barbecue hung over Morningside for days. Genevieve's garden was nothing more than a muddy field of hoofmarks.

A kangaroo and a deer lurking in the hall cupboard proved to be an Armani jacket and a Jil Sanders coat bought in a Harvey Nichols' sale.

'You had a jacket made from kangaroo skin?' her mother said. 'How extraordinary. Did it have pockets?'

On the wind-up radio, Melanie warned people about the illegality of hoarding livestock or buying swans' eggs on the black market.

Genevieve wondered if it was illegal to hoard moths.

A flock of geese flew, on lumbering wings, around the living room. Some of them barged into the windows and fell like sandbags onto the bare, carpetless floor. Genevieve shooed them out of the front door and watched them take off into the sky. Upstairs, her Siberian goose-down duvet from John Lewis had vanished into thin air. A few white feathers drifted slowly on the draught of air from the unsealed window.

In the kitchen, the linoleum on the floor had been replaced by a field of cotton. In the cupboards, instead of plates and cups there were lumps of clay. Where there had been table linen in the drawers there was now flax sprouting. Genevieve's mother arrived with her spinning wheel.

The moths still remained. Inedible, neither toiling nor spinning, merely decorative. 'We could kill them and pin them into pretty shapes,' her mother suggested.

'No,' Genevieve said. 'Let's not do that.'

Genevieve and her mother walked into town. They couldn't stay in Genevieve's house. Where the furniture had once been was a small forest, and the floors were carpeted in a litter of prehistoric zooplankton and algae that felt like biscuit crumbs underfoot. 'What is that?' her mother asked and Genevieve said, 'All the plastic stuff, I think.'

'Back to nature,' her mother said. 'Everything reverting back to where it came from?'

'Looks like it,' Genevieve said.

'Are you doing this?'

'Apparently.'

They walked across the Meadows and over George IV Bridge. A small contingent of moths followed at a discreet distance. As they passed the Bank of Scotland headquarters on the Mound, the windows fell out and turned to quartz and the walls disintegrated into great piles of sandstone.

'Maybe you should have stayed indoors,' Genevieve's mother said as they watched the North Bridge rattling down into its constituent elements. The spine of the old town collapsed. Buildings everywhere turned back into rock and haematite and water and other things that made Genevieve wish she had paid more attention in chemistry classes at school.

'Who knew there was so much rock?' Genevieve's mother said. 'Have you noticed that there are no people? Anywhere.'

'What do you think happened to them?' Genevieve said.

'I don't know,' her mother said. 'Where do people come from?' Later, the night sky gave an answer. Thousands upon thousands of new constellations, brighter than electricity. Genevieve could swear that she could make out the contours of Melanie's face in one of them.

'How does that Joni Mitchell song go?' Genevieve's mother murmured.

'We are stardust?'

'That's the one.

It didn't take long for everything to grow back green. Plants rambled over the ruins, creatures bounded and crept and swam and flew and tried to keep out of the way of Genevieve's mother's small, sharp, silver knife. Civilisation disappeared, 'Back to the garden,' Genevieve's mother said. 'And that's a good thing. Although I miss gin. And a good orthopaedic mattress.'

'Do you think we're gods or something?' Genevieve mused.

'Wouldn't we know if we were?'

'What should we do about the future? Will I have to mate with the animals?' Genevieve tried to imagine herself in the heartless clutches of a bear, a tiger or the infamous wolfkin. She'd had some terrible boyfriends in the past. Perhaps it wouldn't be so bad.

The bleak midwinter had been replaced by a permanent balmy midsummer. Peach trees reached their branches out to them, offering lush fruit; ripe apples dropped at their feet; they stumbled on melons. Moths flitted enigmatically around.

'I really don't know what the future holds,' Genevieve's mother said, 'but you're the garden designer. I suppose you'd better get on with designing a garden. But the whole Adam and Eve thing? I'd give it a miss if I were you.'

Genevieve picked up an apple that had fallen at her feet and peeled it with her mother's small, sharp, silver knife. The apple peel spiralled like a helter-skelter to the ground and turned into a snake that slithered away into the long, green grass beneath an apple tree.

'OK,' she agreed. 'No people this time.'

Fieldwork

IAN RANKIN was born in Fife in 1960. His first Rebus novel was published in 1987, and the Rebus books are now translated into thirty-one languages. He is the recipient of four Crime Writers' Association Dagger Awards and in 2004 won America's celebrated Edgar Award, for *Resurrection Men*. He has also presented a TV series, *Ian Rankin's Evil Thoughts*. He lives in Edinburgh, with his partner and two sons.

Of his Ox-Tale, Ian Rankin says: 'I penned this story at the behest of the Hay Festival. They were looking for stories of exactly 200 words' duration, and I can seldom resist a challenge. I've tweaked it slightly, because when I ran a word count it turned out I'd written 202 words!'

'A GOOD AGRICULTURAL SMELL,' Rebus muttered. It was an August evening, the sun sinking. The field had been ploughed, but there was no sign of manure. Edinburgh's pathologist, Professor Gates, was crouching over the body of local farmer Dennis Maclay. Rebus peered over his colleague's shoulder.

'Head's been smashed,' he stated.

'Not to mention the urine – whole body's drenched in it.'

Which explained the smell. Rebus looked around. 'Animals?' he guessed.

'Human.' Gates stood up. 'I've seen some things in my time ...'

Rebus lit a cigarette. 'How long since it happened?'

'I'd say a good twelve hours.'

'Was he dead when ...?'

'He'd have put up a fight, otherwise!'

Rebus could see crows circling the trees at the edge of the field. It was so peaceful out here, six miles west of the city, the motorway a distant drone. Suddenly there was a roar directly overhead: the outline of a passenger jet, making its approach to the airport.

'Professor,' Rebus said quietly. 'You know those stories? Blocks of ice falling from aircraft, jettisoned from the toilets …?' Now Gates raised his eyes, following the plane's progress. 'Hot day like this, how long would it take for something like that to thaw …?'

The Importance of
Having Warm Feet

MARINA LEWYCKA was born of Ukrainian parents in a refugee camp in Kiel, Germany in 1946. She moved with her family to England and now lives in Sheffield, where she lectures at Sheffield Hallam University. Her debut novel *A Short History of Tractors in Ukrainian*, appeared in 2005 and has been translated into more than thirty languages. It was followed by *Two Caravans* (2007) and *We Are All Made of Glue* (2009).

WHEN NAPOLEON'S SOLDIERS RETREATED in chaos from the burnt-out ruins of Moscow in the winter of 1812, and tried to beg their way back to France, some stragglers wandered southwards through the frozen marshes of Pripyat to turn up, mad with hunger and cold, with cracked lips and frost-bitten feet, in the snow-bound villages of Ukraine. They would knock on the doors, and plead, 'For the love of God, give me refuge, mon ami.'

The villagers called them 'monamishchiki'. Some took pity and brought them in, sat them by the fire, and fed them beetroot soup. But it was no good. Once the gangrene had set into their frost-black toes, it was followed soon by a killer fever. Of some 500,000 who had set off to conquer Russia, barely 10,000 made it back to France.

And it was all because of unsuitable footwear, my great great-great-grandmother told my great-grandmother, who told my mother, who told me.

And snuggled up in front of the coal fire in our two-up-two-down terrace in Bradford, listening to the wind and sleet hammering on the door, my heart went out to those poor frozen-footed refugees.

My mother dressed me up warmly for school. I wore a grey woollen coat buttoned up to the chin, with mittens threaded through the sleeves on a long piece of elastic, and a striped knitted scarf, and sensible lace-up shoes and grey woollen socks that came up to my knees. For, said Mother, we have a saying in Ukraine: 'Keep your head cool, your belly hungry, and your feet warm, and you will live a hundred years on God's earth.'

'The main thing is the feet – keep your feet warm,' said Mother, and gave me a big hug and a little shove to propel me through the gates of St Christopher's Primary School into the mass of kids milling in the playground. 'And work hard, and always listen to the teachers.'

The other kids laughed at my sensible shoes and woollen socks. They sniggered at my long plaits, and my funny name, and my brand-new school satchel. I burned with secret shame, but I pretended not to notice. I wanted more than anything to fit in – no, to *blend* in, to be invisible.

My chief tormentors were two lads called Roger Biggins and Colin Crouchley. I feared them. They would creep up behind me and pull my hair or run off with my satchel. Roger

Biggins was scrawny and mean with a permanently runny nose. Colin Crouchley had a high whinnying laugh that got all the other kids laughing too.

'Take no notice,' Mother said. 'Work hard, and listen to the teachers. Once you have a good education and a good job, you will be the one to laugh at them.'

The form teacher, Mrs Turlow, was a stout bossy woman with a loud voice, a large bosom and dyed golden hair. There was no messing about in *her* class. She played the piano at assembly, sitting upright on the narrow stool, her feet working up and down on the pedals, her muscular wrists poised dramatically above the keys for a moment before crashing down – plonk plonkety plonk – 'Sing up, F3! I can't hear you!'

Obediently, I sang up: *'Jesus bids us shine with a pure clear light.'*

Roger Biggins smirked and winked at Colin Crouchley, who leaned forward and tugged my plait.

'Like a little candle, burning in the night,' I shrilled.

'Like a likkle candle!' whinnied Colin Crouchley. There was a buzz of suppressed giggles. Mrs Turlow stopped, her wrists suspended in the air, and swung around on her stool. Silence fell.

'*Some* children', she said, 'are being *very* silly. I *hope* I'm not going to have to say this *again*.'

Plonk plonkety plonk.

MARINA LEWYCKA

Everybody sang: *'In this world is darkness, so we must shine.'*

'Is everybody shining?' bellowed Mrs Turlow. 'I want to see everybody shining!'

'You in your small corner, and I in mine.'

I liked Mrs Turlow. I felt safe in her classes. I shone. Where Roger Biggins and Colin Crouchley couldn't get me, I buried myself among the books in the reading corner and explored the mysterious world of Janet and John.

But my favourite teacher was Miss Stapleton, who taught Scripture. She was tall and wispy, with silver hair tied back in a bun, and large yellow teeth.

'Ukraine!' she said in our first lesson. 'How fascinating! And are your family Orthodox or Catholic?'

'I'm not sure, Miss. I'll ask.'

But when I asked my father, he laughed.

'We were brought up to believe in Diamat. Dialectical Materialism.'

'Don't talk such nonsense!' said Mother. 'Orthodox. Tell your teacher we are Orthodox.'

'Please Miss, my mother is Orthodox, and my father is Dialectical Materialism.'

'Dialectical Materialism! How fascinating!' said Miss Stapleton. 'Perhaps you can tell us all about it one day.'

For a while, I lived in dread that I would be called upon to explain Dialectical Materialism. One day I saw Miss

Stapleton looking at me with a kind little smile, and when she caught my eye she winked. Then I knew I never would.

At the beginning of December we started to practise for the end of year Nativity Play, and I was chosen to be the Virgin Mary.

'For what were Mary, Joseph and Baby Jesus, if not refugees?' said Miss Stapleton, with her kind yellow-toothed smile.

Mother was proud when I told her I'd been chosen.

'It's because you worked hard and listened to the teachers,' she said, giving me a hug. I didn't tell her that I thought a different principle was in operation, for Roger Biggins, who never worked hard or listened to the teachers, had been chosen to be Joseph. And Colin Crouchley was to be the innkeeper.

I was to wear Mrs Turlow's ample pink nightgown, tied in with a curtain tassel round the waist, and Miss Stapleton's blue tablecloth on my head. Roger Biggins wore his father's striped dressing gown, and a tea towel on his head.

'You look lovely,' Mother said, as she pinned the table-cloth under my chin. 'Just like the Virgin Mary in the icon at St Michael of the Golden Domes. But it's December, and the school hall will be cold. What will you wear on your feet?'

'I can't wear those big black shoes,' I said. 'They'd look stupid.'

'No,' Mother agreed, 'the Virgin Mary wouldn't wear shoes like that. But she would need to keep her feet warm on such a long journey. Just wear the socks.'

Mother was right. It was cold in the school hall, even though the big cast-iron radiators had been on all day. The parents trooped in and sat in rows on the child-sized chairs. In the wings there was a frenzy of excitement as Mary and Joseph and the three wise men and the six shepherds, and the eight angels, and the ox and the ass and the piglet (don't ask) and the innkeeper and his wife all struggled to get into their costumes. You couldn't move for tea towels, table-cloths, nighties, dressing gowns, net curtains, tinsel and safety pins.

'Lovely, dear!' said Miss Stapleton, straightening my tablecloth. But Mrs Turlow spotted the socks.

'Did the Virgin Mary wear grey woolly socks?' she boomed. 'I think not.'

'But Miss …'

But Mrs Turlow was already adjusting Joseph's tea towel. And hadn't Mother told me always to obey the teachers? I took off the socks, and shoved them into my satchel, which was hanging with my coat in the hall.

Then Mrs Turlow seated herself at the piano, raised her stout wrists into the air and brought them down on the keys.

'*In the bleak midwinter,*' the choir of angels sang, '*frosty winds did moan.*'

It was my cue. I came onto the stage, leaning on Joseph's arm.

'Oh, Joseph, my dear, I am so weary and so cold. Where will I lay my head tonight?'

'*Earth stood hard as iron ...*'

'Do not worry, Mary. Look, here is an inn.'

'*Snow had fallen, snow on snow. Sno-o-ow on snow ...*'

There was a commotion in the hall. A figure jumped up in the middle of the third row, and pushed herself past the knees of the seated parents towards the door.

'Isn't that your mum?' whispered Roger Biggins slyly.

'Oh, please, Joseph. Knock on the door!' I replied.

Roger knocked on the wooden stage door, but before the innkeeper could answer, someone burst onto the stage and rushed up to me. In her hands was a pair of grey woolly socks.

'Put them on at once!' my mother exclaimed. 'You'll catch your death of cold!'

The music stopped. The action stopped. Everyone in the hall watched with bated breath as I bent down, wobbling on one foot then the next, and pulled the socks on under Mrs Turlow's nightgown.

'That's better,' whispered Mother, so loud that even the

people at the back could hear. Then she disappeared into the wings.

The piano started up again. The choir sang.

'In the bleak midwinter lo-o-ong ago!'

I stood and watched, paralysed, as my mother resumed her seat in the audience.

'Oh, oh, my baby's coming!' Roger Biggins whispered into my ear.

'What?'

'You're supposed to say, 'Oh, oh, my baby's coming!'

'Oh, oh, my baby's coming!'

The innkeeper appeared at the door. It was Colin Crouchley.

'Oh, who is this?' he exclaimed. Then, pausing for dramatic effect, 'My, what a lovely pair of socks!' He laughed his high whinnying laugh, and the whole hall erupted in laughter. The shepherds laughed. The choir of angels laughed, the three wise men laughed. Even the ox and the ass and the piglet laughed. Only the Virgin Mary didn't laugh. She stood silently amid the laughter, and a tear rolled down her cheek.

Then Miss Stapleton tiptoed onto the stage and brushed away the tear with a corner of the tablecloth, and Mrs Turlow struck up on the piano again.

'Ding dong merrily on high!'

A little while later, Baby Jesus was laid in the manger at St Christopher's Primary School and the Virgin Mary dried her tears and went home with her mother.

I never forgave my mother for that until her dying day, but on her dying day I forgave her.

It was December, too, and there was snow on the ground outside. Mother was propped up in bed in the downstairs room, lying quite still, because every movement brought a spasm of pain, despite the morphine the doctor had prescribed.

I sat by the bed, holding her hand, and talking to keep her mind away from the pain. And when the pain got too bad for memories to blot out, I fed her a little more morphine on a spoon.

'My dear,' she whispered, pulling my hand to bring my cheek down close to hers, 'my feet are so cold. I think I'm going to die soon.'

'Shhh! I'll find you some socks.'

I rifled through the chest of drawers in her bedroom, and found a pair of pink fluffy bed socks, and reaching under the blanket pulled them onto her cracked swollen feet, gently, so as not to disturb her pelvis, where the cancer lay.

'Ah, that's better.'

And that simple action suddenly opened the door on a memory some fifty years old.

'Do you remember the school play, Mother, when I was the Virgin Mary, and you came onto the stage and made me put on a pair of warm socks?'

'Did I do that? How terrible.'

'It doesn't matter. I'd forgotten all about it.'

'When you're a parent you try to do everything that's right for your children, then later you find that you did it all wrong.'

'You did everything right,' I said, and kissed her cheek. 'It mattered then, but it doesn't matter now.'

Mother died later on that afternoon. I held her hand as it turned cold in mine, and a tear rolled down my cheek. But I was glad, too, that when she stepped out on her last long march into the cold unknown, at least her feet were warm.

Hanif KUREISHI

Long Ago
Yesterday

HANIF KUREISHI was born and brought up in Kent and read philosophy at King's College, London. He is the author of numerous novels, short story collections, screenplays and plays. In 1984 he wrote *My Beautiful Laundrette*, which received an Oscar nomination for Best Screenplay. *The Buddha of Suburbia* won the Whitbread Prize for Best First Novel in 1990. His second novel, *The Black Album*, was published in 1995 and his first collection of short stories, *Love in a Blue Time*, in 1997. *Intimacy*, his third novel, was published in 1998, and was adapted for film in 2001. A film of his most recent script, *Venus*, directed by Roger Michell, was released in 2007. His latest novel is *Something to Tell You* (2008). Hanif Kureishi lives in west London.

ONE EVENING JUST AFTER my fiftieth birthday, I pushed against the door of a pub not far from my childhood home. My father, on the way back from his office in London, was inside, standing at the bar. He didn't recognise me but I was delighted, almost ecstatic, to see the old man again, particularly as he'd been dead for ten years, and my mother for five.

'Good evening,' I said, standing next to him. 'Nice to see you.'

'Good evening,' he replied.

'This place never changes,' I said.

'We like it this way,' he said.

I ordered a drink; I needed one.

I noticed the date on a discarded newspaper and calculated that Dad was just a little older than me, nearly fifty-one. We were as close to equals – or contemporaries – as we'd ever be.

He was talking to a man sitting on a stool next to him, and the barmaid was laughing extravagantly with them both. I knew Dad better than anyone, or thought I did, and I was tempted to embrace him or at least kiss his hands, as I used to. I refrained, but watched him looking comfortable at the bar beside the man I now realised was the father of a school friend of mine. Neither of them seemed to mind when I joined in.

Like a lot of people, I have some of my best friendships with the dead. I dream frequently about both of my parents and the house where I grew up, undistinguished though it was. Of course, I never imagined that Dad and I might meet up like this, for a conversation.

Lately I had been feeling unusually foreign to myself. My fiftieth hit me like a tragedy, with a sense of wasted purpose and many wrong moves made. I could hardly complain: I was a theatre and film producer, with houses in London, New York and Brazil. But complain I did. I had become keenly aware of various mental problems that enervated but did not ruin me.

I ran into Dad on a Monday. Over the weekend I'd been staying with some friends in the country who had a fine house and pretty acquaintances, good paintings to look at and an excellent cook. The Iraq war, which had just started, had been on TV continuously. About twenty of us, old and young men, lay on deep sofas drinking champagne and giggling until the prospect of thousands of bombs smashing into donkey carts, human flesh and primitive shacks had depressed everyone in the house. We were aware that disgust was general in the country and that Tony Blair, once our hope after years in opposition, had become the most tarnished and loathed leader since Anthony Eden. We were living in a time of lies, deceit and alienation. This was heavy, and our lives seemed uncomfortably trivial in comparison.

Just after lunch, I had left my friend's house, and the taxi had got me as far as the railway station when I realised I'd left behind a bent paper clip I'd been fiddling with. It was in my friend's library, where I'd been reading about mesmerism in the work of Maupassant, as well as Dickens's experiments with hypnotism, which had got him into a lot of trouble with the wife of a friend. The taxi took me back, and I hurried into the room to retrieve the paper clip, but the cleaner had just finished. Did I want to examine the contents of the vacuum? my hosts asked. They were making faces at one another. Yet I had begun to see myself as heroic in terms of what I'd achieved in spite of my obsessions. This was a line my therapist used. Luckily, I would be seeing the good doctor the next day.

Despite my devastation over the paper clip, I returned to the station and got on the train. I had come down by car, so it was only now I realised that the route of the train meant we would stop at the suburban railway station nearest to my childhood home. As we drew into the platform I found myself straining to see things I recognised, even familiar faces, though I had left the area some thirty years before. But it was raining hard and almost impossible to make anything out. Then, just as the train was about to pull away, I grabbed my bag and got off, walking out into the street with no idea what I would do.

Near the station there had been a small record shop, a bookshop and a place to buy jeans, along with several pubs that I'd been taken to as a young man by a local bedsit aesthete, the first person I came out to. Of course, he knew straight away. His hero was Jean Cocteau. We'd discuss French literature and Wilde and pop, before taking our speed pills and applying our makeup in the station toilet, and getting the train into the city. Along with another white friend who dressed as Jimi Hendrix, we saw all the plays and shows. Eventually I got a job in a West End box office. This led to work as a stagehand, usher, dresser – even a director – before I found my 'vocation' as a producer.

Now I asked my father his name and what he did. I knew how to work Dad, of course. Soon he was more interested in me than in the other man. Yet my fear didn't diminish: didn't we look similar? I wasn't sure. My clothes, as well as my sparkly new teeth, were more expensive than his, and I was heavier and taller, about a third bigger all over – I have always worked out. But my hair was going grey; I don't dye it. Dad's hair was still mostly black.

An accountant all his life, my father had worked in the same office for fifteen years. He was telling me that he had two sons: Dennis, who was in the Air Force, and me – Billy. A few months ago I'd gone away to university, where, apparently, I was doing well. My all-female production of *Waiting for Godot* – 'a bloody depressing play', according to Dad – had been admired. I wanted to say, 'But I didn't direct it, Dad, I only produced it.'

I had introduced myself to Dad as Peter, the name I sometimes adopted, along with quite a developed alternative character, during anonymous sexual encounters. Not that I needed a persona: Father would ask me where I was from and what I did, but whenever I began to answer he'd interrupt with a stream of advice and opinions.

My father said he wanted to sit down because his sciatica was playing up, and I joined him at a table. Eyeing the barmaid, Dad said, 'She's lovely, isn't she?'

'Lovely hair,' I said. 'Unfortunately, none of her clothes fit.'

'Who's interested in her clothes?'

This was an aspect of my father I'd never seen; perhaps it was a departure for him. I'd never known him to go to the pub after work; he came straight home. And once Dennis had left I was able to secure Father's evenings for myself. Every day I'd wait for him at the bus stop, ready to take his briefcase. In the house I'd make him a cup of tea while he changed.

Now the barmaid came over to remove our glasses and empty the ashtrays. As she leaned across the table, Dad put his hand behind her knee and slid it all the way up her skirt to her arse, which he caressed, squeezed and held until she reeled away and stared at him in disbelief, shouting that she hated the pub and the men in it, and would he get out before she called the landlord and he flung him out personally?

The landlord did indeed rush over. He snatched away Dad's glass, raising his fist as Dad hurried to the door, forgetting his briefcase. I'd never known Dad to go to work without his briefcase, and I'd never known him to leave it anywhere. As my brother and I used to say, his attaché case was always attached to him.

Outside, where Dad was brushing himself down, I handed it back to him.

'Thank you,' he said. 'Shouldn't have done that. But

once, just once, I had to. Suppose it's the last time I touch anyone!' He asked, 'Which way are you going?'

'I'll walk with you a bit,' I said. 'My bag isn't heavy. I'm passing through. I need to get a train into London but there's no hurry.'

He said, 'Why don't you come and have a drink at my house?'

My parents lived according to a strict regime, mathematical in its exactitude. Why, now, was he inviting a stranger to his house? I had always been his only friend; our involvement had kept us both busy.

'Are you sure?'

'Yes,' he said. 'Come.'

Noise and night and rain streaming everywhere: you couldn't see farther than your hand. But we both knew the way, Dad moving slowly, his mouth hanging open to catch more air. He seemed happy enough, perhaps with what he'd done in the pub, or maybe my company cheered him up.

Yet when we turned the corner into the neat familiar road, a road that had, to my surprise, remained exactly where it was all the time I hadn't been there, I felt wrapped in coldness. In my recent dreams – fading as they were like frescoes in the light – the suburban street had been darkly dismal under the yellow shadows of the streetlights, and filled with white flowers and a suffocating, deathly odour, like being buried in roses. But how could I falter now? Once inside the house, Dad threw open the door to the living room. I blinked; there she was, Mother, knitting in her huge chair with her feet up, an open box of chocolates on the small table beside her, her fingers rustling for treasure in the crinkly paper.

Dad left me while he changed into his pyjamas and dressing gown. The fact that he had a visitor, a stranger, didn't deter him from his routine, outside of which there were no maps.

I stood in my usual position, just behind Mother's chair. Here, where I wouldn't impede her enjoyment with noise, complaints or the sight of my face, I explained that Dad and I had met in the pub and he'd invited me back for a drink.

Mother said, 'I don't think we've got any drink, unless there's something left over from last Christmas. Drink doesn't go bad, does it?'

'It doesn't go bad.'

'Now shut up,' she said. 'I'm watching this. D'you watch the soaps?'

'Not much.'

Maybe the ominous whiteness of my dreams had been stimulated by the whiteness of the things Mother had been knitting and crocheting – headrests, gloves, cushion covers; there wasn't a piece of furniture in the house without a knitted thing on it. Even as a grown man, I couldn't buy a pair of gloves without thinking I should be wearing Mother's.

In the kitchen, I made a cup of tea for myself and Dad. Mum had left my father's dinner in the oven: sausages, mash and peas, all dry as lime by now, and presented on a large cracked plate, with space between each item. Mum had asked me if I wanted anything, but how would I have been able to eat anything here?

As I waited for the kettle to boil, I washed up the dishes at the sink overlooking the garden. Then I carried Father's tea and dinner into his study, formerly the family dining room. With one hand I made a gap for the plate at the table, which was piled high with library books.

After I'd finished my homework, Dad always liked me to go through the radio schedules, marking programmes I might record for him. If I was lucky, he would read to me, or talk about the lives of the artists he was absorbed with – these were his companions. Their lives were exemplary, but only a fool would try to emulate them. Meanwhile I would slip my hand inside his pyjama top and tickle his back, or I'd scratch his head or rub his arms until his eyes rolled in appreciation.

Now in his bedwear, sitting down to eat, Dad told me he was embarked on a 'five-year reading plan'. He was working on *War and Peace*. Next it would be *Remembrance of Things Past*, then *Middlemarch*, all of Dickens, Homer, Chaucer, and so on. He kept a separate notebook for each author he read.

'This methodical way,' he pointed out, 'you get to know everything in literature. You will never run out of interest, of course, because then there is music, painting, in fact the whole of human history—'

His talk reminded me of the time I won the school essay prize for a tract on time-wasting. The piece was not about how to fritter away one's time profitlessly, which might have made it a useful and lively work, but about how much can be achieved by filling every moment with activity! Dad was my ideal. He would read even in the bath, and as he reclined there my job was to wash his feet, back and hair with soap and a flannel. When he was done, I'd be waiting with a warm, open towel.

I interrupted him. 'You certainly wanted to know that woman this evening.'

'What? How quiet it is! Shall we hear some music?'

He was right. Neither the city nor the country was quiet like the suburbs, the silence of people holding their breath.

Dad was holding up a record he had borrowed from the

library. 'You will know this, but not well enough, I guarantee you.'

Beethoven's Fifth was an odd choice of background music, but how could I sneer? Without his enthusiasm, my life would never have been filled with music. Mother had been a church pianist, and she'd taken us to the ballet, usually *The Nutcracker*, or the Bolshoi when they visited London. Mum and Dad sometimes went ballroom dancing; I loved it when they dressed up. Out of such minute inspirations I have found meaning sufficient for a life.

Dad said, 'Do you think I'll be able to go in that pub again?'

'If you apologise.'

'Better leave it a few weeks. I don't know what overcame me. That woman's not a Jewess, is she?'

'I don't know.'

'Usually she's happy to hear about my aches and pains, and who else is, at our age?'

'Where d'you ache?'

'It's the walk to and from the station – sometimes I just can't make it. I have to stop and lean against something.'

I said, 'I've been learning massage.'

'Ah.' He put his feet in my lap. I squeezed his feet, ankles and calves; he wasn't looking at me now. He said, 'Your hands are strong. You're not a plumber, are you?'

'I've told you what I do. I have the theatre, and now I'm helping to set up a teaching foundation, a studio for the young.'

He whispered, 'Are you homosexual?'

'I am, yes. Never seen a cock I didn't like. You?'

'Queer? It would have shown up by now, wouldn't it? But I've never done much about my female interests.'

'You've never been unfaithful?'

'I've always liked women.'

I asked, 'Do they like you?'

'The local secretaries are friendly. Not that you can do anything. I can't afford a professional.'

'How often do you go to the pub?'

'I've started popping in after work. My Billy has gone.'

'For good?'

'After university he'll come running back to me, I can assure you of that. Around this time of night I'd always be talking to him. There's a lot you can put in a kid, without his knowing it. My wife doesn't have a word to say to me. She doesn't like to do anything for me, either.'

'Sexually?'

'She might look large to you, but in the flesh she is even larger, and she crushes me like a gnat in bed. I can honestly say we haven't had it off for eighteen years.'

'Since Billy was born?'

He said, letting me caress him, 'She never had much enthu-siasm for it. Now she is indifferent ... frozen ... almost dead.'

I said, 'People are more scared of their own passion than of anything else. But it's a grim deprivation she's made you endure.'

He nodded. 'You dirty homos have a good time, I bet, looking at one another in toilets and that ...'

'People like to think so. But I've lived alone for five years.'

He said, 'I am hoping she will die before me; then I might have a chance ... We ordinary types carry on in these hateful situations for the single reason of the children and you'll never have that.'

'You're right.'

He indicated photographs of me and my brother. 'Without those babies, there is nothing for me. It is ridiculous to try to live for yourself alone.'

'Don't I know it? Unless one can find others to live for.'

'I hope you do!' he said. 'But it can never be the same as your own.'

If the mortification of fidelity imperils love, there's al-ways the consolation of children. I had been Dad's girl, his servant, his worshipper; my faith had kept him alive. It was a cult of personality he had set up, with my brother and me as his mirrors.

Now Mother opened the door – not so wide that she could see us, or us her – and announced that she was going to bed.

'Good night,' I called.

Dad was right about kids. But what could I do about it? I had bought an old factory at my own expense and had converted it into a theatre studio, a place where young people could work with established artists. I spent so much time in this building that I had moved my office there. It was where I would head when I left here, to sit in the café, seeing who would turn up and what they wanted from me, if anything. I was gradually divesting myself, as I aged, of all I'd accumulated. One of Father's favourite works was Tolstoy's 'How Much Land Does a Man Need?'

I said, 'With or without children, you are still a man. There are things you want that children cannot provide.'

He said, 'We all, in this street, are devoted to hobbies.'

'The women, too?'

'They sew, or whatever. There's never an idle moment. My son has written a beautiful essay on the use of time.'

He sipped his tea; the Beethoven, which was on repeat, boomed away. He seemed content to let me work on his legs. Since he didn't want me to stop, I asked him to lie on the floor. With characteristic eagerness, he removed his dressing gown and then his pyjama top; I massaged every part of him, murmuring 'Dad, Dad' under my breath. When at last he stood up, I was ready with his warm dressing gown, which I had placed on the radiator.

It was late, but not too late to leave. It was never too late to leave the suburbs, but Dad invited me to stay. I agreed, though it hadn't occurred to me that he would suggest I sleep in my old room, in my bed.

He accompanied me upstairs and in I went, stepping over record sleeves, magazines, clothes, books. My piano I was most glad to see. I can still play a little, but my passion was writing the songs that were scrawled in notebooks on top of the piano. Not that I would be able to look at them. When I began to work in the theatre, I didn't show my songs to anyone, and eventually I came to believe they were a waste of time.

Standing there shivering, I had to tell myself the truth: my secret wasn't that I hadn't propagated but that I'd wanted to be an artist, not just a producer. If I chose, I could blame my parents for this: they had seen themselves as spectators, in the background of life. But I was the one who'd lacked the guts – to fail, to succeed, to engage with the whole undignified, insane attempt at originality. I had only ever been a handmaiden, first to Dad and then to others – the artists I'd supported – and how could I have imagined that that would be sufficient?

My bed was narrow. Through the thin ceiling, I could hear my father snoring; I knew whenever he turned over in bed. It was true that I had never heard them making love. Somehow, between them, they had transformed the notion of physical love into a ridiculous idea. Why would people want to do something so awkward with their limbs?

I couldn't hear Mother. She didn't snore, but she could sigh for England. I got up and went to the top of the stairs. By the kitchen light I could see her in her dressing gown, stockings around her ankles, trudging along the hall and into each room, wringing her hands as she went, muttering back to the ghosts clamouring within her skull.

She stood still to scratch and tear at her exploded arms. During the day, she kept them covered because of her 'eczema'. Now I watched while flakes of skin fell onto the carpet, as though she were converting herself into dust. She dispersed the shreds of her body with her delicately pointed dancer's foot.

As a child – even as a young man – I would never have approached Mother in this state. She had always made it clear that the uproar and demands of two boys were too much for her. Naturally, she couldn't wish for us to die, so she died herself, inside.

One time, my therapist asked whether Dad and I were able to be silent together. More relevant, I should have said, was whether Mother and I could be together without my chattering on about whatever occurred to me, in order to distract her from herself. Now I made up my mind and walked down the stairs, watching her all the while. She was like difficult music, and you wouldn't want to get too close. But, as with such music, I wouldn't advise trying to make it out – you have to sit with it, wait for it to address you.

I was standing beside her, and with her head down she looked at me sideways.

'I'll make you some tea,' I said, and she even nodded.

Before, during one of her late-night wanderings, she had found me masturbating in front of some late-night TV programme. It must have been some boy group, or Bowie. 'I know what you are,' she said. She was not disapproving. She was just a lost ally.

I made a cup of lemon tea and gave it to her. As she stood sipping it, I took up a position beside her, my head bent also, attempting to see – as she appeared to vibrate with inner electricity – what she saw and felt. It was clear that there was no chance of my ever being able to cure her. I could only become less afraid of her madness.

In his bed, Father was still snoring. He wouldn't have liked me to be with her. He had taken her sons for himself, charmed them away, and he wasn't a sharer.

She was almost through with the tea and getting impatient. Wandering, muttering, scratching: she had important work to do and time was passing. I couldn't detain her any more.

I slept in her chair in the front room.

When I got up, my parents were having breakfast. My father was back in his suit and my mother was in the uniform she wore to work in the supermarket. I dressed rapidly in order to join Dad as he walked to the station. It had stopped raining.

I asked him about his day, but couldn't stop thinking about mine. I was living, as my therapist enjoyed reminding me, under the aegis of the clock. I wanted to go to the studio and talk; I wanted to eat well and make love well, go to a show and then dance, and make love again. I could not be the same as them.

At the station in London, Father and I parted. I said I'd always look out for him when I was in the area, but couldn't be sure when I'd be coming his way again.

Telescope

JOANTHAN BUCKLEY was born in Birmingham, and has written both fiction and travel guides (for Rough Guides). He lives in Brighton with his wife and son. His first novel, *The Biography of Thomas Lang*, was published in 1997, followed by *Xerxes* (1999), *Ghost MacIndoe* (2001), *Invisible* (2004) and the critically acclaimed *So He Takes the Dog* (2006). His new novel, *Contact*, will be published in 2009. 'Telescope' is from a novel-in-progress about 'an absolute outsider'.

CHARLIE THINKS HE HAS FOUND the right person: Ellen Symons, forty-two, professional carer, recently separated, obviously capable, immediately likeable and available right away. Janina thought she was lovely, says Charlie, and we both know that this is an adjective used sparingly by Janina, and very rarely upon first acquaintance. 'What do you think?' he says, producing a photo. The face is plain and pleasant enough, but I can't say that loveliness radiates from it – she looks kindly, slightly bemused (understandable, in the circumstances) and extremely tired. I'd have guessed somewhere nearer fifty than forty. If he's happy I'm happy, I tell Charlie. He's definitely happy, he assures me: Ellen was their clear first choice. It turns out, however, that she's the only choice. Candidate number one, upon being shown a snap of the invalid, said, 'I'm sorry, no, I can't,' and departed so quickly it was as if Charlie had pulled down his pants in front of her. The next put her hand to her mouth and said nothing for a full minute, before similarly excusing herself. Another suggested that, in view of what was being asked of her, the remuneration should be revised upwards to the tune of one hundred percent. Only Ellen passed the test of full disclosure impressively. 'Gosh,' she murmured, but regained her balance right away. Within a minute they were discussing the arrangements. Janina brought her upstairs to see the room that would be hers and the room where the patient will die. She stayed for coffee.

My new lair has been decorated and shelves have been erected. Not enough shelves – a lot of stuff will have to go into the loft. Can't complain, however. Charlie has a photo of the room, and it all looks very nice. If I change my mind about the white, some colour can be introduced – Janina thinks it's too cold, but if white is what I want, white it shall be. He even has a photo of the view from my future window, and this looks nice too: fields, distant low hills, a lot of sky. Janina is taking care of the logistics of the removal. She'll oversee the packing, the re-routing of the mail, meter readings, and so on. 'My wife could have run the Berlin airlift single-handed,' says Charlie. He collects a takeaway and we watch TV for a couple of hours.

Goodbye to Sandra, and not a wet eye in the house. 'I'll miss you,' she tells me, giving the pigsty one last long look of

farewell as she buttons her coat. Next week she'll be attend-
ing to the needs of a decrepit old gentleman in Forest Hill:
there'll be some incontinence to deal with, and she's expected to push him around the streets for an hour or two every
day, but she's not anticipating any behavioural issues and
the pay is better. He used to have a big job in the City so he's
got a bit of cash stashed away, but he's gay so he's got no
children to look after him, which she thinks is one of the sad
things about being that way, when you get older and there's
no kids to look out for you. Yes, gay isn't the right word, I
sadly concur. She's glad I'm moving to the semi-countryside.
'Fresh air, a change of scene, having the family with you –
it'll be better than here,' she says. I'm sure she's right, I
answer, before presenting the final envelope. Assessing the
size of the bonus by touch, she wishes me good luck. 'Thank
you,' I say. I promise I'll write to her. 'That'd be nice,' she
replies. From the door she gives me a wave, like a released
prisoner at the gates.

An operatic dawn to welcome me: pale peach sun behind
miles-wide rungs of amber cloud; fields and trees daubed
with diluted honey; in the background, low undulations of
indigo hills; jubilant blackbirds. At 5.30 a.m. a garage door
slides open as smoothly as an eyelid, releasing a vast black

BMW, the first commuter out of the blocks. A few minutes later there's a Mercedes sliding down the slipway of a long stone-paved drive, turning slowly onto the empty street. It's another hour before the station-bound people appear in force: a sudden posse, mostly men, moving right to left. There's even a wife in a front garden, waving the spouse on his way. By 8 a.m. the flow has ceased, more or less. Some smaller cars, driven by women, take to the streets; half a dozen buggy-pushers pass by; the chug of a digger begins, on a site that would appear to be a short distance beyond the right-hand limit of the visual field.

A tractor, listing severely, traverses an expanse of soft dun soil. With not a thought in my head, I'm watching it return when Charlie comes in, bearing breakfast. I assure him that I slept well, which I did. Charlie reiterates that I must treat the house as my own. 'We don't want you spending all day up here,' he says, and at this moment there's a knock and in comes Janina, smiling with such delight you'd have thought she'd feared she might have found me dead in my bed. Behind her stands my hired companion.

Ellen is a considerably larger lady than I had imagined from the photo, and the eyes, dark grey, have a less weary cast than they did in the picture. The slabby upper arms are squeezed by the sleeves of a dress that's patterned with flowers in various shades of lilac, mauve and purple; big white buttons hold it tightly to a big white chest. The shoes aren't right for the ensemble: block-like black things with a ridge around the toes and thick crêpe soles – nurse's footwear. It's evident that my mugshot didn't do me justice, either. 'Pleased to meet you, Mr Brennan,' she says, blinking too rapidly. 'Oh Christ,' she's thinking, 'this chap looks like something that's melted.' Charlie is pushing a chair forward for her, and she glances at it as if having to remind herself what a chair is for. Janina withdraws. 'Not looking my best today,' I say to Ellen. 'You won't mind if I don't kiss you?' It will take her some time to adjust to the mumbling, but she gets the gist and gives me a queasy smile. Charlie remains with us for ten minutes, having sensed that Ellen may be regretting her decision. Taking charge, he runs through a brief agenda of housekeeping topics: the medication schedule, questions of diet and hygiene. Could the furniture, he asks me, be redeployed in ways more useful to me? All is hunky-dory, I reply. Ellen has the look of a learner driver on her first lesson, waiting for the instructor to turn the ignition key. When I request sandwiches for lunch she concentrates as though committing a code number to memory. If I need anything, I'm to use the buzzer. 'Anything at all,' says Charlie, with much nodding from Ellen.

On the stroke of 1 p.m. Ellen is at the door with a plate of sandwiches. Cheese and bread have been aligned to a tolerance of one millimetre, and the butter has been spread evenly and thinly into every angle of every slice. 'Is there anything else I can do for you?' she asks. 'Shall I stay for a while?' There's a wariness that suggests she's been warned of a brittle temper. 'I'm fine, thank you,' I reply. 'You're sure?' she asks. I tell her that I am quite sure, and she leaves it at that. At three o'clock, on the dot, she's back: she helps me get up, freshens the bed, dispenses the pharmaceuticals, brings over a couple of books. A tautness around the mouth and jaw betrays the effort of suppressing repugnance; she doesn't chatter. Talk is limited mostly to discussion of the evening meal, which is brought punctually at seven, with a big mug of tea made exactly to specifications. She smiles as she places the mug on the table, remarking that she's never known anyone drink tea so weak. It was like making a martini, she says: she just introduced the tea to the water for a second, like letting the gin get a sniff of the vermouth. She glances at me, trying to assess my reaction. You have to look hard to read my face, because the skin isn't telling you anything, and she can't be sure that her familiarity was appropriate. I begin to understand why Charlie was so taken with her. 'I have a refined palate,' I inform her. I suspect she hears: 'I have a fine parrot.'

At ten she comes to wash me, our last interaction of the day. Very lightly she runs a flannel over my skin. I can see her, reflected in the taps, turning aside as if for air. 'Is this all right?' she asks from time to time. It is: she performs the task with the concentration and delicacy of a bomb-disposal expert. When she closes the door she does it as softly as you'd close the door of a room with a sleeping baby in it.

An ironing board, with an iron on it, has been standing in the bedroom window of a house across the street for three full days now. From time to time I see someone in there; at night the curtains are closed and a light shines through them – so the room is being used. The head of the bed is against the far wall. So, as they lie in bed, looking towards the window, the occupants see the iron standing to attention, awaiting its next pile of clothes. Depressing.

Again the dream of the walled lawn – the third or fourth time in the past month. As it begins, there is a strong and pleasurable sensation of recognition, but I have no idea of what is going to be seen. The centre of the scene is a sizeable and irregular area of grass, cut as closely as a bowling green, with a high brick wall around it and trees rising behind. It is dusk, and it appears to be a warm evening: people in summer dresses and short-sleeved shirts are standing around the edge of the grass, talking with the air of guests who are waiting for an event to happen. Someone or something is going to appear over the lip of the slope that falls away at the far end of the green, where previously there had been a wall. Beyond this slope can be seen the lights of a town, not far away, but full night has fallen there, while on the lawn it's still dusk. Nobody arrives; nothing happens. In a murmur the people continue to talk; the atmosphere of anticipation leaks away, but everyone seems perfectly content to remain there, talking in the constant dusk. A feeling enters the dream: it seems that whatever was going to happen has in some way, imperceptibly, happened. The trees look like oaks; sometimes there's a tent, a white marquee, which has the aura of a memory, but I don't think I've ever seen it.

When Ellen comes in I ask her: 'Do you have interesting dreams, Ellen?' She is a little surprised, perhaps by the question, perhaps because I've used her name for the first time. She's been calling me Daniel for a few days now.

'Not often,' she replies. 'Shops. I dream about shops quite a lot, and buying food I don't like, or clothes that aren't right. They're not the right size, not the right colour or something, but I have to buy them for some reason.' I can tell she can tell that my face is smiling as clearly as is possible for it. Recently she dreamt about being alone at night in a supermarket where the aisles were so long she couldn't see the end of them. She was walking and walking and walking, pushing an empty trolley, and there was hardly anything on the shelves, just a can here, a box there, a few bottles. 'It was so boring I couldn't bear it,' she says. 'I bored myself awake.' Here I laugh. The sound is more like a cough, but she knows it's a laugh.

I show her what I've written, about the people on the grass. 'What do you think it means?' she asks and I start to tell her that it doesn't mean anything, that it's just something that happened in my head – but I'm incomprehensible, so I write it out for her. 'You see wonderful things when you're asleep,' I say to her, 'but you aren't really seeing, are you? It's enjoyable, but it's not really you that's enjoying it.'

She frowns. 'I don't know about that,' she says, 'but I wouldn't mind having dreams like I used to have when I was a girl. But your brain's losing its fizz when you get to our age, isn't it?'

'Try these,' I suggest, tapping a bottle of tablets, and for a moment, I'm sure, she thought I meant it.

What have we learned today? That it was in the Harajuku district of Tokyo, in the mid-1990s, that young people first began to combine elements of traditional Japanese dress – the *kimono*, the *obi*, *geta* sandals – with custom-made clothes and cast-offs and designer gear. One of the multitudinous styles that arose at this time was *decora*, in which clothes were hung with toys and plastic jewellery that made a light noise as the wearer walked. Also popular was the 'elegant gothic Lolita' look, which added black lace, corsets and other vampy accoutrements to the well-established 'Lolita' style. Many young women modelled their attire on cartoon characters such as the Sailor Senshi of *Sailor Moon*, one of the most successful creations in the 'magical-girl' sub-genre of *anime* and *manga*, in which young girls combat the forces of evil with their superhuman powers. Here's a twenty-ish girl wearing a red tartan mini-kilt, fat-soled red vinyl boots, a faux-leopardskin stole and a T-shirt hooped with bands of a dozen different colours. Another photo shows six young women who appear to be going for a paedophilic group-sex fantasy kind of look: pigtails; tiny pink miniskirts; huge shaggy boots; hooped candy-bright tights; supertight Minnie Mouse T-shirts. The monthly magazine *FRUiTS*, established in 1997 by photographer Shoichi Aoki, is essential reading for those interested in the latest developments in Harajuku.

Janina brings me the phone – it's Stephen, with an incident. A profusely bearded man, wearing a full-length black cape fastened around the neck with a thick golden chain, climbed aboard the bus this morning. This gentleman was also wearing, on this blustery and overcast day, a huge pair of sunglasses, of a style one would associate with Jackie Onassis. And he was sucking on the stem of a pipe. There was no pipe – just a stem. Cape-man sprang on board, and inevitably planted himself next to Stephen. He removed the sunglasses, turned to face Stephen, and smiled benignly. He wanted Stephen to understand that plumes of some ethereal substance – invisible to all but this improbable adept – were dancing on the heads of everyone around them. The reason he had seated himself next to Stephen, he explained, was that Stephen's efflorescence was a remarkable bipartite thing, with one large indigo plume and a much smaller scarlet one alongside. Such bifurcated head-flames were very rare, and in all the years that had passed since the man was granted the gift of being able to discern the plumes, he had never seen one of such beautiful coloration. 'Very, very lovely,' he said, and then he removed himself to the upper deck.

'Remember the mauve lady?' asks Stephen. Indeed I do: the woman with mauve shoes, mauve tights, mauve coat, mauve dress, mauve plastic bangles (about twenty of them), mauve earrings, mauve eyeshadow (lots of it). Having sat beside him without comment all the way from Oxford Circus to Brixton, she suddenly asked, demurely, sweetly: 'How old do you think I am?' Stephen, knocking fifteen years off the lowest plausible age, answered, 'Sixty?' The old lady blinked, as though he were a doctor who'd just broken the news that she was going to expire within the week, and yelled to the driver that she wanted to get off, right away.

Wafts of slow thick drizzle since reveille; the sky a panel of old zinc across its whole extent; fields obscured by grey wash; hills invisible. Janina brings the telescope that my parents gave to Peter for his tenth birthday. 'I thought this might be useful,' she says. I thank her, thinking: 'For what, exactly?' Putting Peter's book of British birds on my table, she tells me there are herons down by the stream. For more than an hour I shun the thing, but then I find myself scanning the farmland and soon, in a gap in the mist, I spot a fox, rain-blackened, dithering on the edge of the copse. For a whole minute it stands there, considering the dullness, before retreating to the undergrowth. A Land Rover emerges from between the hedgerows of the lane to the farm: when I get it in my sights I see the driver, a middle-aged man, being harangued by his passenger, a scrawny gent in his seventies, who brings his face to the windscreen and bares his teeth at the murk. The woman who waves goodbye to her husband every morning emerges from her house, with trenchcoat belted, huge umbrella aloft and a scarf over her hair – not a look one sees very often nowadays. A heron flies over the hedges on the south side of the farm. Later there's a glimpse of a raptor – a kestrel, I think. In the direction of the ridge there is now the beginnings of a fissure in the cloud, a streak of paler greyness like a trickle of meltwater seen through thick ice. Here, however, we have rain: the quiet chortle of water in the drainpipe is the only sound, other than the occasional evidence of Janina about her business downstairs. Oh yes, there can be no very black melancholy to him who lives in the midst of nature and has his senses still.

Janina and Charles, Ellen reports, would like me to spend more time with them. Perhaps this evening we could all eat together? I appreciate the offer, I answer, but this evening I have other plans. She tells me how much she likes my brother and his wife: they've really made her feel like one of the family. I'm very pleased to hear it.

'Perhaps tomorrow evening?' she asks.

'Perhaps tomorrow evening what?'

'You could come downstairs.'

'We'll see.'

'They really would like it,' she goes on. There's more on the kindness of Janina and Charlie; much use of 'really'.

'They are saints, but I'm tired,' I tell her. 'Please leave me alone.' She goes without a word, like an actress following the director's orders.

The state of Minnesota has some 15,000 lakes and its name means 'sky-tinted water'. ('From the waterfall he named her, / Minnehaha, Laughing Water.') The state bird is the Common Loon, *Gavia immer*, otherwise known as the Great Northern Diver. The state butterfly is the Monarch, the state fish the Walleye, and the state flower the Pink and White Showy Lady's Slipper. A roll-call of eminent Minnesotans: Bob Dylan, F. Scott Fitzgerald, Judy Garland, Charles Lindbergh, Prince, Charles Schulz.

By way of an apology, I ask Ellen if her accommodation is to her liking. 'It is,' she replies, briskly removing the sheets from the bed. Eye contact so far has been perfunctory. She tells me that she and Janina are going to redecorate the room at the weekend.

'So you're not planning on leaving before me?' I ask.

'No,' she states. 'I'm not.'

I ask if the music bothers her.

'Sandra warned me,' she answers.

I'd had no idea that she'd been debriefed by her predecessor; I want to know more.

'She said you like to have noise around you,' says Ellen.

'Noise?' I roar, faux-furious, but as I'm making the sound I realise that only I can tell it's fake. 'It's Scarlatti, for crying out loud.' This comes out as gibberish: the ulcers are really making a mess of the enunciation.

'What?' asks Ellen.

I point to the CD box. 'What else did Sandra tell you?'

'Nothing much,' says Ellen.

This cannot be true. 'Tell,' I say.

'She said she could never understand how you could read with a radio on, and another radio blaring next door.'

I point out that when you walk down the street there's stuff going on all around you: people talking, music coming out of cars and shops, and while all that's going on you're seeing adverts and glimpses of newspapers and magazines and TVs in shop windows. 'Think of it as an indoor street,' I tell her.

It takes a while for me to say this, and Ellen listens attentively, frowning, as if listening to someone to whom English does not come easily. When I've finished, she says: 'But you don't read in the street, do you?'

'OK. But you read in the park, no?'

'Suppose so,' she says, unpersuaded, smoothing the fresh bedlinen.

'Sandra hated this stuff,' I tell her. She knows Sandra hated it. 'What about you?' I ask.

'Sounds like a mad person throwing cutlery down the stairs,' she says. 'I'll go and get your breakfast.'

Ambroise Paré on the meaning of dreams: 'Those who abound with phlegm dream of floods, snows, showers and inundations, and falling from high places ... Those who abound in blood dream of marriages, dances, embracings of women, feasts, jests, laughter, or orchards and gardens.'

The quartet dines together, and Charlie produces a fine bottle of Burgundy to mark the occasion. I dribble profusely; the food – a nice-looking assemblage of chicken fillets and pine nuts and raisins and rice, over which Janina has worked for hours, no doubt – tastes of oatmeal. Ellen cuts up my portion of meat with the minimum of fuss. Conversation sporadic and unrelaxed; I'd rather be in my room. Charlie is giving Ellen a summary of his day at the office when the doorbell rings. Janina answers, and returns two minutes later, nicely flushed. The caller was some horrible woman who wants to become a local councillor, she says. There's a rumour that the council is going to be taking a lot of asylum seekers, and this woman thinks our money should be spent on better things – things that benefit us, the community. Janina called her a Nazi and sent her away with a flea in her ear. 'There are so many people like that around here,' Janina informs Ellen. 'They want the government to crack down on the immigrants, but they're happy to pay a Polish girl a pittance to keep their house spick and span.' Charles gives her a light slap on the shoulder. 'That's my girl,' he says, pulling a face of comic alarm. 'My wife likes a scrap,' he says, 'but I'll do anything for a quiet life. Mr Risk-Averse, that's me.' Janina says this isn't true – he'd taken risks with the business, and they'd paid off. A brief passage of affectionate bickering ensues, for Ellen's benefit.

Ellen out for an hour in the morning, to meet Roy, the ex-husband. They have one or two things to discuss; nothing major, she says. She suggests that I might like to sit in the garden, as it's such a nice day. I stay in my room instead, reading in the chair by the window. At twelve I see Ellen at the end of the road; viewed through the telescope, her face suggests that the encounter has not gone well. 'Everything OK?' I enquire, when she brings in the lunch.

'Fine,' she says.

'Not how it looked,' I say.

'That's just the way the face hangs,' she answers. 'It's all going south.'

'Tell me.'

'There's nothing to say.'

It's obvious that she and Roy argued. 'Tell me, please,' I wheedle. 'Come on, tell me,' I go on, irritatingly.

'That's enough, Daniel,' says Ellen. 'Behave.'

Tanizaki writes that the Japanese sensibility prefers tarnished silver to polished, the shadowy lustre of jade to the crass glitter of precious stones. The gold decoration of Japanese lacquer-work, he says, must be seen in candlelight, not in the glare of electricity.

Ellen is drying my back and I notice, reflected in the window, her gaze slipping over the skin. A wince of pity, and I can almost hear the question being whispered: 'I wonder who you'd be if you didn't look like this?' Answer: 'Well, I wouldn't exist, would I?'

I tell her about the count and countess, a long time ago in Italy, who had a daughter who was a dwarf. They raised her in a house in which all the staff were dwarves, and never allowed her out, so she grew up thinking that her parents were giants. Not sure if I've read this story or made it up. The former, I think.

The Death of Marat

NICHOLAS SHAKESPEARE (born Worcester, 1957) grew up in the Far East and South America. After a stint making documentaries for the BBC, he joined *The Times* and then became literary editor of the *Daily Telegraph* and *Sunday Telegraph*. A winner of the Somerset Maugham and Betty Trask prizes, he has written five novels, including *The Dancer Upstairs* (which was filmed by John Malkovich), and an acclaimed biography of Bruce Chatwin. His latest novel is *Secrets of the Sea* (2007), set in Tasmania, where since 1999 he has lived for part of each year. He is currently editing Bruce Chatwin's letters.

WHO IS DILYS HOSKINS? A 55-year-old widow with white hair and sharp blue eyes that look out from unintendedly fashionable horn-rims. The mother of two children, both now in their twenties. Widowed for eight years. Born on the east coast of Africa in a country of high-duned beaches, deep lakes, fertile plains, intractable marshes and deserts. A woman to whom the following words might apply were you to speak with neighbours in her run-down apartment block: detached, resourceful, a hard barterer, ladylike. In other words, a most improbable assassin.

She is at the end of her long month in London. Her daughter Rachel has just given birth to Dilys's first grand-child, an eight-pound boy with a piercing cry. Dilys has been staying in the converted basement of Rachel's terraced house in Putney, helping out. In five days' time, she will fly to Australia for her son Robin's graduation ceremony, from his school of architecture in Perth, before returning to her one-roomed flat in her African capital, into which she moved after the government confiscated Coral Tree Farm. She does not deny the surplus of fear that spills out when she considers the chaos that awaits her, or the poisonous sense of her own impotence. She is only one untrained person. What can she do to help? She is not a nurse, not a doctor; she is a farmer's wife who for the past eight and a half years has wanted a husband and a farm. But her mind is made up.

Her children have been emailing each other. They don't think that she should return. She has a strained relationship with both.

On a rainy evening in the last week of her visit, Dilys stands in her daughter's kitchen, waiting for a pot of tea to brew, when she hears Rachel call in an urgent voice: 'Mum, you've got to come. He's on the telly.'

The word 'he' burns on her breath.

Dilys impatiently fills two mugs, then takes them into the living room where, seated on a large sofa beside her breastfeeding daughter, she watches, over her tea, the still-boyish features of her president denying the epidemic.

It is a novelty for Dilys to observe how outsiders report on her country. There is no one to contradict the President from within. Foreign journalists are forbidden. When Dilys is at home, her short-wave radio is jammed to blazes. Russia says nothing; China is just as feeble. But here on the BBC there are regular news items.

'Nay, there is no epidemic,' the President insists in his mission-school, old-fashioned English, jabbing his forefinger at an appreciative crowd. It is a rumour put about by the nefarious white minority with the Europeans and Americans behind them. It is the Europeans and Americans who are responsible for the food queues, the fuel queues; who even now are intercepting vital oil supplies on the high seas and scheming to recolonise the country with the assistance of greedy racist usurpers ... He is dressed in his signature blue kaftan and a white baseball cap which looks ridiculous perched on top of his thick black shock of hair.

Rachel listens to the hectoring voice. Her baby, unlatched momentarily from its breast, gives a small air-sucking convulsion, then reclamps its gums around the dark purple bullet of her nipple.

Neither Dilys nor Rachel says what's on their mind. The words have been used over and over:

You malignant bungler. Only one man is responsible for reducing the country to ruin; everywhere the stink of death, disease gnawing its way from village to village, farms deserted, motherless children grovelling for food through stacks of uncollected garbage; and night after night the pick-axe handles rising and falling, the bloodshed, the mutilations, the rapes, the abductions. One man, Mr Pointer.

What her daughter does say: 'I've had another message from Robin. He says you're mad. You've got a round-the-world ticket – all you have to do is keep flying till you get back to London and I'll pick you up again at Heathrow.'

Dilys swallows another watery sip of Darjeeling and says nothing.

Irked, Rachel cradles her baby. 'I know it's hard, Mum. It was our home, too.'

She lapses into silence. She has a blonde fringe and her father's small chin. Then, in a reasonable voice: 'Listen, I've spoken again to Tim about the basement. It's not what you're used to, but you'd have your own entrance.'

'Robin is getting quite serious about this Australian girl?' with great firmness.

'For God's sake, Mother!'

Rachel's emotions are running very close to the surface. She is, however, an old hand at manipulating her mother.

Dilys slams down the mug. 'I am going back, Rachel,' in a flaming tone. 'And nothing you, Robbie or your husband can say will stop me. It's where I belong.'

Her ferocity shakes them both. Arms folded, she sits at a perpendicular angle and watches her daughter cover the baby's ears, shielding it from the shouting.

'What is wrong with you?' Rachel hisses, and turns the child towards the television screen, giving it an uninterrupted view of an embroidered blue kaftan and a brushed-up halo of black hair. She prepares to leave the room. 'Where does this anger come from? You can be angry, but not *that* angry.'

Next morning, to avoid the stress of another argument, Dilys borrows Rachel's umbrella and leaves the already cramped house and waits for a bus to take her to Piccadilly. It's a midsummer morning, but the rain has not stopped since she arrived in London. At last, a bus sloshes to a halt. When a teenage boy – white and spotty, with wires trailing from under his woollen cap – attempts to barge past her onto it, she grabs his arm. 'Excuse me.'

She elbows her way ahead of the boy to buy her ticket and is mildly astonished to be told that the fare is the same as a week ago. She gives the driver the right coins and a grateful, shaky smile, and pockets her ticket and moves along to the rear of the bus.

Settled into her seat, Dilys feels foolish for having exploded. She sits back and casts her eye around the other passengers. The faces are white, black, brown, yellow – and mostly British, presumably. As the bus crosses the Thames, she floats the opinion that what she is seeking is reassurance. She is looking for someone like her. Because isn't what she faces merely the lot of all 55-year-old women of a 'certain generation' who have disappeared on themselves in the quicksand of domestic life?

She gazes out over the river at the dark mob of clouds assembled in the London sky. But the tunnelling mole of her anger hasn't gone away.

When Dilys was a young mother, her friends called her 'Sleeping Beauty'. A feisty and rather plump child, she had had the handicap of a late-blooming beauty. Suddenly to find herself at twenty-eight turning heads was almost more disorienting to her than the birth of her first child, which followed closely after. Overnight, along with the extra weight that had insulated her, she lost her pluckiness and confidence. With the arrival of cheekbones, she became benign, mild-mannered, accommodating. Now Dilys – she who flies off the handle at the tiniest provocation – has repossessed her childhood ferocity. Other people might think that she has turned into someone new, but they are quite wrong. You can't remake yourself into who you are not. On the other hand, you can return to the person you once were. She is simply stretching the muscles, dormant for so long, of the unruly girl.

Four impervious rows ahead, the teenager watches the rain-spattered window, swaying his head from side to side.

Thirty-five minutes later, Dilys steps down opposite the Ritz and is walking past the Royal Academy, feeling cold and wet and oppressed, when she notices on the railing a framed poster for a Munch exhibition and is reminded of the reaction on her daughter's face the night before. Dilys can't recall her last visit to an art gallery. Her fine white hair twinkling with raindrops, she collapses her umbrella and goes in.

The painting hangs in the furthest room. Dilys doesn't see it at first. Her eyes glide dutifully from wall to wall and then her heart stops. A face looks out at her, into her – sparking a shock of recognition.

It's hard for Dilys to explain, this giddying affinity she feels for the young woman with tangled yellow hair. The small breasts and swollen belly remind her of the desperate black girls in her East African capital. But the pale colour of the skin – squeezed fiercely from the tube and painted in rapid horizontal brushstrokes, like slashes – is her own. The colour of celery, white clock towers, pith helmets.

Only closer up does she see that the young woman is not alone: stretched out on a bed behind her, also naked, is a man with a moustache.

Dilys fumbles with her audio-guide and learns from a dispassionate voice that the man is the French revolutionary leader Marat; and the woman – who has gained access to Marat on the pretext of revealing a plot against him – Charlotte Corday. 'Munch completed the work in 1907, a year before his breakdown ...'

The subject of the painting surprises Dilys. The two figures are so modern, like lovers in a bedsit. And, while she has heard of Marat, she knows nothing about Charlotte Corday – except that she famously stabbed Marat in his bath. She definitely wasn't in the painting by Jacques Louis David. Who is she? How did she kill him?

She lifts her head and meets the stare of the assassin. The expression is vacant, corpse-like (even the dead man on the bed seems more alive), but it goes on snatching at Dilys.

Some time later, Dilys steps back from *The Death of Marat*. The painting has entered her marrow. The signalling emptiness of the young woman's face, its aura of aloneness, confronts Dilys with the bleaching of the canvas of her own existence. She feels boiling over all the things that she can't – or won't – discuss with Rachel and Robin. They are the one family link left, but their thrust to start again, to build new lives in Britain and Australia, has deafened her children. Dilys knows the pattern too well – she has taught it to them: In order to survive, you have to forget. You have to. But her oblivion, so painstakingly achieved, is unravelling.

As she walks back to the cloakroom, the outsized feeling takes hold of Dilys to challenge one of these people entering the Royal Academy: 'Are you aware that my president thinks you are supposed to be enjoying an unholy alliance with a few defenceless farmers who live in another continent?'

She'd expect shrugging shoulders. 'Sorry, the situation sounds ghastly,' as they shove past. And over the shoulder, 'Didn't you choose to stay? Isn't that what happens in Africa?' Or, if they know some history, 'Isn't he simply taking back land seized by whites in the 1890s?'

In her obstinate mind she runs after them, shakes them, violated by their indifference. 'I'm sorry, but did you know that eight out of ten of these 'settler vermin', my late husband included, bought their farms *since* independence – that is to say, *under the President's very own laws?*'

There is so much that she would like to get off her chest. She could stand here and talk all week and there'd be plenty left over. But how fast the blinds rattle down whenever she tries to explain – her parents had not come out until after the early days, when they were busy killing people; she does not carry a gun; did not call her dog after the President or sing, 'Climb the hill, baboon'. She is not one of those excruciating 'whenwes', who begin each backward-groping conversation 'When we lived in ....' But even though she isn't one of those, Africa is the only place she knows. She is an African just as much as her president is. Britain owes her nothing. All she has in common with the original pioneers – and with some of the crowd in the Munch exhibition – is the whiteness of her skin.

One person who understands is a mad, dead Norwegian painter. In the catalogue, she reads that Munch said he was pregnant with his painting *The Death of Marat* for nine years.

Dilys is not due to leave for Australia until Friday evening. Tingling with the novelty of being truly herself, she will spend her remaining afternoons in London in the Putney library, digging out books on the French Revolution.

Charlotte Corday arrived in Paris on a blazing July afternoon, battling her way through crowds all dressed in tri-coloured cockades and soft liberty caps, and booked into the Auberge de Provence, a stuffy first-floor room overlooking the Rue des Vieux Augustins. The porter put down her bulging leather bag and without saying anything drew open the heavy curtains. The nosy summer sunshine picked out a marble-topped desk and an unmade bed. She turned to the porter, a big-boned man, slightly deaf with a box jaw that hung open, and asked him to fetch a chambermaid to make up the bed and then to bring her a pen, ink, some paper.

That afternoon, she set down the words she had rehearsed in her head on the journey from Caen. She wrote quickly, no crossings out. The peace of France depended on the fulfilment of the law. She was not breaking it by killing a man who had been so universally condemned. If she was guilty, then Hercules too was guilty when he killed Geryon and Cacus. But did Hercules ever meet a monster so odious?

She folded the sheet six times and pinned it to her baptismal certificate.

This was the conviction she had reached: Marat had to be killed and peace restored.

No one is so strong as the woman who stands alone. She had asked nobody for help, breathed not a word of her plan to anyone. Those who knew her imagined she was in England. Before departing Caen, she had written to her father: 'I am going to England because I do not believe one can live happily and quietly in France for a very long while to come.'

A whole nation can pay for the folly of one man. She was going to restore peace to the world by ridding it of a monster.

Who is this Dilys Hoskins who is so infatuated with Charlotte Corday and is now seated in the economy-class cabin on the overnight flight to Singapore? A woman in her imperfections and vanities not markedly different from any other passenger. Not a hero as a consequence of her determination to stay put, but a menopausal widow with nowhere else that she wants to go – except home. A woman who has no answer to the question: At what point are you entitled to feel part of the land where you were born; at what point do you earn your stake in its living earth?

She glances at the young couple in her row, engrossed in their film. Do you know what is going on, how bad? If you do not know, how can you help? But if you knew how bad it was, would you be able to help?

The newspaper in her lap tells her that the epidemic is spreading, aggravated by the rains. There is a photograph of an empty hospital, the wards deserted. Two children sit on the steps waiting for their parents to show up. The President has not been seen in public for several days.

'The tragedy', says a representative from an aid agency, 'is that this disease is deadly but curable.'

Her hard-headed husband once said to her with red-dened eyes in the days after they lost their farm: 'I would do it, given the chance.'

'I know you would, darling,' she said and squeezed his hand as he had grabbed hers at the start of her labour with Rachel, and two years later with Robin.

That's how deep it was with Miles – he wouldn't vote again for the President to save his soul from hell. But his cancer went deeper.

Her meal tray cleared and the overhead lights switched off, Dilys tries to sleep. But her feet are swelling up and a shadow flitting from side to side across the back of her mind is preventing her.

Charlotte Corday woke early on that hot Saturday morning in July, and put on a simple brown dress of piqué cotton, a white linen fichu that she tucked into her bodice, a black hat. All very quiet and sober.

It was 7.30 a.m. when Madame Grollier, the hotelier, unlocked the front door to let her out. The shops were not yet open. She reached the Palais Royal within twenty minutes and went for a walk around the public gardens. The plants were shrivelled and coated in dust. She made ten circuits and then left the gardens and walked up the Galeries de Bois to number 177, where a burly man was pulling open the shutters. In the window she spotted a display of cutlery. The man, Monsieur Barbu, the shop's owner, invited her in. She was looking for a kitchen knife, she told him; something to pare fruit with. He took out a velvet-lined tray and she chose a black-handled knife with a six-inch steel blade. The handle was carved from ebony and had two rings on it – and he demonstrated how it might be hung from a shelf or a cook's belt. She paid forty sous for the knife, which came in a green leather sheath, and slid it into her pocket, and thanked him and walked out.

On her way back to the gardens, she bought a newspaper and sat on a green bench to read it. The news from Orléans was that nine men were to be guillotined following an attempt to murder Marat's deputy. She put down the newspaper, the breath pushed out of her. At that moment a small boy running past fell over. He yelped in pain and looked up at her, chin wrinkling, his face pressed to the path. Their eyes met and, though from a different angle, each saw that the other wanted to cry, and perhaps because of this recognition both held back from actually doing so. She helped the boy to his feet and stroked his apple-red cheek, smiling, a small grave smile of sadness, and he stumbled off, rubbing the gravel from his knees, with an exaggerated limp.

'Black Robespierre' is what they had called him, some of the farmers she grew up with. The same ones who fled abroad after his election. 'You wait, Dilys,' as they packed their belongings. 'Beneath that preposterous kaftan, there'll always be a Mao collar.' She wanted not to argue, but believe. She was in her mid-twenties then, Rachel's age, and had faith in the President and the vision he articulated for their (yes, their) country in his shy, polite, wedding photographer's voice. These farmers were taking the Yellow Route out, she couldn't help thinking. She went to one of their yard sales and bought a Black & Decker drill with some bits missing and a Zenith short-wave transistor radio.

And how reasonable the President appeared at the outset. All that stuff about forgiveness, his passion for peace, of wanting to take everyone with him. The President wanted the whites to stay, help rebuild. There would be no retribution, a little redistribution maybe, in time; but revenge, nay, not that. He appoints a white farmer as his agricultural minister to safeguard the farmers' future. He listens attentively, in his blue kaftan. He has a new name: Mr Pointer, the people call him with affection – because he always points his finger when speaking. He's a messianic figure. Everyone wants to meet him.

So her husband takes Mr Pointer at his word. Her husband in his floppy green hat who loved lemon cream biscuits and fine-shredded marmalade and the tangos of Carlos Gardel. Who saw the worst in everyone only after he had seen the best. One always admires the qualities in people that one lacks oneself. Miles's assertive manner was the

same towards everyone. A man whose unbelievable blunt-
ness went hand in hand with an extreme honesty. When
they met, he was the owner of a thriving printer's shop on
the capital's main street, but with a hankering for the land:
land that Mr Pointer with outstretched arms was urging
people such as Miles to take up.

'The secret of success in life', Miles tells Dilys as if she
were his apprentice and not his wife, and as she would later
tell their children, 'is to be ready when your opportunity
comes – and go for it.' He sells his printing business and with
their joint savings they buy a small tobacco farm twelve miles
inland from the sea. They invest in a herd of milk-producing
cows. They install a new hand-pump in the chicken-yard
to draw up water from the aquifer. They renovate the
house, a modest whitewashed single-storey building at
the top of a long lawn hedged with thorn bushes in which
plum-coloured starlings like to nest, and a view beneath
a thrilling sky over a horizon tufted with elephant grass.
The sandy soil needed plenty of fertiliser, but the river
gave water all year round. She would watch her children
slide down the water-smoothed rocks and go exploring
with them on an escarpment veined with an ancient stone
terrace.

She needs to be useful. She starts up a school, employ-
ing two teachers; she creates a library for the village; she

ensures that the workers have a nice place to live in. To use her president's words, she is doing her best 'to move forward together'. She has grown up playing with African children. It doesn't always make you a non-racist, but in her case the strong feelings that they all form part of one scrappy tribe have stayed. Although she is never so assertive or abrupt as her husband, she treats Africans as does Miles, as she would Europeans, and they like her for it. They notice that Sleeping Beauty is increasingly picking up her husband's ways, but at least they know that when she is being rude to them she would behave no differently towards white people. Everyone waves at her when she drives around – unlike at the next property, where the farm workers glower.

Dilys was educated in the capital in the same school as her mother. In her French class she studied Camus. She envied him when he wrote, 'This earth remains my first and last love.' At Coral Tree Farm, she learns to understand Camus's sympathy for the land. During harvest time, she is never out of the tobacco shed. Each time she grades a leaf and rubs the ribbed arteries beneath the tips of her fingers, she feels an immediate connection with those who have cropped the plant and with the soil that has produced it; an involvement which passes beyond intimacy. The tobacco leaf, like the warm frothing milk that she squeezes from the cows, is tangible, something she can pinch and smell. It is life itself.

Unlike her liberal friends, Dilys is unsentimental about Africans; she has seen enough to know that Africa is a tough place – the Troubles have taught her that. But it's only when living on the farm that she experiences the authentic sense of Africa being *her* place. As though a book she is reading in another language has shifted imperceptibly into her language.

At what point did the truth come tumbling down on her that Black Robespierre had diddled – Miles's word – his people? At what point did the bluebottle settle on the lens to reveal that the President's promise of integration was just a fiction? Specifically, at what point did the quiet, shy, friendless wedding photographer become the raucous shock-haired demagogue in a baseball cap, urging his thugs to turn on settler vermin like the Hoskins family? In other words, at what point did Mr Pointer decide to punish her for the white taint of her skin?

The questions are like the furious horizontal strokes of Munch's brush.

The driver of the hackney cab in the Place des Victoires had no idea where Marat lived and had to climb down and amble along the rank asking his colleagues. '30 Rue des Cordeliers,' one of them yelled. 'Just off Faubourg Saint-Germain.' He heaved himself back up and shortly before eleven o'clock dropped her off outside a tall grey shabby house with shops on either side.

Charlotte walked through an empty porch into a courtyard where two women chatted in the shadow of an arcade.

She asked: 'Citizen Marat?'

'Staircase on the right,' nodded one of them, her eyes lingering on this fastidiously dressed, rather beautiful young woman with enlarged blue humourless eyes.

She crossed the courtyard and ran up the steps, following the iron balustrade to the top of the staircase. The bell pull was a curtain rod with a makeshift canvas handle. She tugged it. Then stepped back, patting down her bodice where she had concealed the knife.

A muffled sound of females talking. Then the door opened and a woman stood there, biting her lip. The disarray in her face mimicked the chaos of the hallway behind. Tiles missing on the floor. Filthy wallpaper – patterned with broken Doric columns. And the rancid smell of over-fried fish.

'What do you want?'

She explained herself in a composed voice. She wanted to meet Marat. It was urgent. She had vital news – about a planned insurrection in Caen.

'Out of the question,' the woman said brusquely. 'Marat is sick. He can't see anyone.'

'What if I come back tomorrow?'

Just then another woman appeared in the doorway: Marat's mistress, Simone. She seconded everything that her younger sister had said. No, she can't make an appointment. It's impossible to say when she'll be able to see him, when he'll be better.

'Then I shall go home and write to him,' she replied calmly, resisting every cell in her body that screamed for her to fight her way beyond them.

Dilys breaks the long flight to Perth with a stopover in Singapore. At the insistence of her son, she is booked for two restorative nights into the Raffles Plaza. The steady hum of the air-conditioning drives out the noise of the city twelve floors below. But she cannot sleep. She wakes and does not know where she is, and for a moment her husband is alive and she is in Africa still.

She is sitting at her tinny little table, trying to lose herself in a novel, when Beauty her housemaid bursts in.

'Mrs Hoskins, you must come …'

Dilys barely keeps up with Beauty as they run to the end of the lawn. She hears the cries from behind the thorn bushes. The cow is stumbling and stopping every few steps, its intestines wrapped around its legs like South American bolas. The grass glistens red from the slashed udders. A head twists around at a strange angle, sensing her presence, and the look in the creature's eyes sends Dilys racing back to the house.

She grabs the keys, her breath coming in short thrusts. She has to kill it. And she doesn't know how. She needs Miles …

The agonised bellows continue to reach her as she struggles to unlock his gun cabinet. Hunting is man's business. But her husband has taken the children for safekeeping to a cousin's house in the capital and will not be back until next day.

She pulls out the rifle and a handful of bullets. She has never killed an animal, other than a chicken when Beauty was away. Miles had infuriated her by saying: 'Don't you worry, I'll do it. You'll never be able to do it,' and she had not let him – she had jolly well halal-killed the chicken exactly as Beauty had taught her.

But a chicken was not a cow.

She stares at the bullets loose in her palm. The same panic has assaulted Dilys ever since Miles's cancer was diagnosed. The panic that tells her he isn't going to be around and she will have to do more and more and she doesn't know how.

That unearthly lowing, it's intolerable.

Through the mesh window – another horrible cry. And she knows in a small, dry, cold and ruthless part of her, in a space beyond the emotions and the histrionics and the tears, that she has no choice. Only she can put the animal out of its suffering. There is only her.

The rifle is unexpectedly light. She walks with a pall-bearer's tread back down the lawn. It isn't that she's unaware of the path she must take. All her life, she has been an observant passenger. But she has never done the driving, and now she has to.

On the other side of the hedge, something is still staggering. A mouth wheezes open and a tongue curls up, stiff, blue, abnormally long. She fumbles and pulls the trigger.

In the dying light, she walks over to the office shed and raises Peter Trasenster on the battery-powered radio. The neighbouring white farmers do a security roll-call every night. Until now the area has been peaceful; their road is the only road into the capital without a curfew. But a fortnight ago, Coral Tree Farm was gazetted in the government newspaper. Ninety days to vacate. Her sick husband is running around calling on lawyers to dispute it.

Trying not to sound melodramatic, she explains to Peter what has happened. He tells her to stay where she is, a local patrol will come by and check. She locks the rifle in the gun cabinet and crosses the lawn and bolts the doors.

Afterwards, no one believed it. Sleeping Beauty – this mild-mannered woman – shooting a cow. Her children were incredulous.

Back in her hotel room, Charlotte Corday manoeuvred the baptismal certificate out from under her breasts, along with the piece of paper attached to it, containing her manifesto. Next, she removed the knife and placed it on the desk behind the ink bottle. She stared at it for a moment, before reaching out and taking a fresh sheet of paper.

Her letter written, she folded it into an envelope, scribbled Marat's name and address on the outside, and rang for the porter. 'Be sure to deliver this by seven o'clock this evening.'

Then she asked Madame Grollier to arrange for a hairdresser to be sent up.

It was something about the sisters, their strong, careless faces. She decided that Marat had a keen eye for women. She was too primly dressed this morning. This time, she would arouse the ex-monk's vanity.

The timid young coiffeur who knocked on her door at 3 p.m. found her waiting for him, already wearing a loose white bombazine gown with a grey underskirt, a low-cut bodice, and over her shoulders a rose gauze scarf. For the next hour he stood behind her, gathering the gold tresses from her round lovely face and braiding them into a single garlic string that fell down the middle of her back.

All this time, she sat there in the solipsism of her conviction, not saying anything. Detached. Her eyes on the marble-topped desk and the knife in its green leather sheath. Absolutely indifferent to what his hands were doing.

He sprayed her hair and throat with cologne and powder.

When she walked downstairs at six-thirty on this baking July evening, it took Madame Grollier a second or two to connect the white-gowned woman who descended in high-heeled shoes, wearing an emerald cockade hat, and fanning her scented face with a gloved hand, and the person who arrived three days earlier from the Normandy countryside with cake crumbs on her sleeve.

Dilys cannot hear them, since bare feet make little noise; and then they are there.

A high-pitched voice draws her from her chair. She parts the curtain and, when she sees who is out there, motions that she is coming. Before leaving the room, she pauses at Miles's desk to pick up something.

The angry voice speaks again as she enters the hall. 'Open this door or we'll fuck you up, *mamma*.'

She unbolts the door and stands in the feeble porch light. Assembled before her, a silent ominous mob stretching back to the tobacco shed. Leather jackets, green caps, red and yellow T-shirts printed with Mr Pointer's smiling face.

A few of the young men carry branches torn from the trees. Others clutch whips made from fan belts and bicycle spokes. Their faces gleam with the prospect of violence.

'What do you want?' addressing their leader. As if she doesn't know.

He raises a golf club. Solidified in its grooved metal head, the mood of menace and uncertainty that has lurked in the background these past months.

'We have come to take your land.'

She runs her eyes over the faces, recognising one.

'Elias?'

When he was a boy, she had bought Elias reading glasses so that he could study.

He looks away.

Disappointed, she turns back to the man holding the golf club. Fresh blood is spattered across his T-shirt. She wonders if it was the cow's blood.

'How old are you?' her eyes angry. Thinking of the cow. She can sense the blue veins standing out on her neck.

The question makes him uncomfortable. He wipes his nose on his leather sleeve.

'Nineteen.'

'Then you were born after the Troubles. That was the year I bought this house ...'

He shakes his arm. 'This land belongs to us. You white Kaffirs came and grabbed it long ago from our people.'

'No, we didn't,' the rebellion rising in her voice. 'I have this certificate from your government' – she has stopped saying 'our' – 'It specifies that it is not needed for resettlement.'

She shows it to him. It will get her nowhere. But she wants him to see it, this annoying young man who all of a sudden has made her feel middle-aged and powerless.

'See there. "No Present Interest". Signed by the courts. *Your* courts,' harping on it.

He frowns at the legal language.

'Mr Pointer makes the law, not the courts.'

'This is still private property. If you don't leave, I shall call the police.'

He laughs. The arrogant, unedited laughter of someone with the sanction of the provincial governor's office. 'The police will do nothing. We can do what we like.' And rips it in half.

Dilys slams the door, bolts it, then seizing Beauty's hand, runs through the house, out the back, to the office shed, thrusting her housegirl down beneath the desk. She's not worried about being raped herself, but the story among the local farmers is that these idiots have been told to rape women like Beauty. To create babies who will vote for Mr Pointer.

Her hands vibrate as she radios the Trasensters. 'Oscar Romeo Four Five.' Across the lawn, she can see the lights being switched on one by one. She listens to the mob thumping on Rachel's harmonium and singing hysterical songs of liberation as they tramp through the rooms. 'We will find you, we will find you …'

'Oscar Romeo Four Five.'

At last, she raises Vanessa Trasenster. 'I need help.'

'Isn't Peter with you?'

'White bitch, where are you?'

A golf club smashes through the panes. Hands stretch through the shattered glass and grope for her hair. A black tentacle fastens around the cable and rips it from the wall. When all of a sudden the baying stops and they are running off, piling onto the tractor with their booty. Car doors slam in the darkness. There's the chatter of a radio. Then Peter Trasenster's voice. 'Dilys?'

In the morning, she walks through the rooms. The children's blackboard broken to bits. Miles's record collection. Her books. Even her son's watch in fragments. And an acrid tang of urine – coming from where, she can't tell.

Mr Pointer's response? 'This is a peaceful demonstration of people who are frustrated.'

Dilys is surprisingly undisturbed by the house invasion. She doesn't perceive it exactly as a tea party at Government House – as one or two neighbours mutteringly suggest – but rather as part of her toughening-up process. What she can't get used to, what unhinges her, is the imminent loss of the farm and the deteriorating effect that this has on Miles. Than her husband no one could be more finicky in the kitchen, but she notes that he has started to leave his knife by the sink, still covered in marmalade.

The hackney cab drew up outside 30 Rue des Cordeliers. She asked the driver to wait and walked in long strides through the porter's lodge – empty as before – and up the stairs.

Her gloved hand tugged on the bell.

The door was swung open by a fat, one-eyed woman, wearing a man's ill-fitting trousers. Visible in the dirty hall-way behind was the pile of newspapers she had been folding – copies of *L'Ami du Peuple*, edited by Marat, and printed on the press which he and Simone had installed in their apartment.

Charlotte started to explain herself all over again.

But the fat woman interrupted. Marat was not seeing anyone. He was taking a bath.

Then would it be possible to find out if Marat has received her letter?

The fat woman glared at her. At the sight of that elegant hair-do and ravishing white bust, a vision of health and privilege, her face contracted. 'Oh, he receives many letters,' and turned to pick up another newspaper. 'Sometimes too many.'

Before anyone could say anything, two men ran up the staircase and barged past. One waved an invoice that required signing. Another had come to take a bundle of newspapers to the War Office.

Angry, she stamped her foot and called out, trying to catch someone's attention. 'I have come from far away with important information that I need to deliver personally to the People's Friend. There's a plot against him. I have names!'

Simone, the mistress, appeared, attracted by all the hubbub. 'Oh, it's you,' momentarily nonplussed by the summer dress and the hat with its knot of emerald ribbons.

'Did he get my letter?'

'Letter? I don't think so.'

'I have to see him.'

'Maybe in two or three days.'

But a man was shouting something from inside the apartment.

Simone excused herself.

She waited, leaning against the wall, watching the fat, one-eyed woman who very deliberately folded another copy of next day's edition of *L'Ami du Peuple*. Charlotte noted with horror that it called for the head of her friend Charles Barbaroux.

Suddenly, Simone was back. 'He will see you.'

Dilys wonders why on earth her son has insisted on her spending two overnights in Singapore, where she knows no one. Unable to sleep, she decides to set out early for a stroll through the city centre.

The humidity hits Dilys the instant she steps outside. She looks right and left before deciding to head off in the direction of Orchard Road. The shops taunt her, their windows filled with filmy sarongs and skirts translucent as flies' wings. Five minutes into her walk and sweat is meandering down her cheeks and neck. She feels disoriented, as if she has stood up in a hot bath. When she comes out into a park with spreading angsana and flame trees, and sees a bench, she flings herself down onto it. All she wants to do is strip.

Dizzy and flushed, she hauls off the burgundy cashmere cardigan that was a gift from her daughter. Her eyes blink with sunshine and sleep and the cardigan clings to her – she had exchanged it for a size smaller because she anticipated shedding the weight she put on in England. She allows it to fall on the bench while she lifts her elbows to let the air circulate. Then fishes inside her bag for a tissue and starts mopping her face.

She is looking about as if she expects the flame trees to lean forward and smother her, when the bench sinks a fraction beneath the weight of another woman.

Her dizziness passes. The park is still again when she falls into polite conversation.

The woman is waiting for her daughter to finish a swimming lesson. She speaks fluent English, but is not English. Tall, slim, mid-thirties, with her light brown hair pulled back and dressed in thin clothes that show her youthful shape, she reminds Dilys of a backpacker who once stayed at the farm. There is something vivacious about her, indiscreet. A woman who likes a good gossip, Dilys senses.

'Are you from here?' Dilys asks, wiping her forehead.

'With a name like Van der Hart!' No, she's Dutch. She has been in Singapore two years. Her husband works for an investment bank; he is in hospital ('an operation for a floating kidney'); he should be home by the weekend ('Fingers crossed – otherwise, I'll have to take him more books!

Barend's always got a book in his hand. I sometimes think he's more interested in books than in me.').

Dilys half-listens, not really engaged. Not accustomed to this humidity. Even sitting down with her cardigan off, she does not feel like herself.

Until Mrs Van der Hart looks at her. 'You're not from here, either.'

'No,' stuffing into her bag the beige-stained Kleenex.

'Are you English?'

She could easily say yes. It's what her children do. Stifling a yawn, she replies, 'No,' and braces herself for the inevitable.

'Where are you from?'

Dilys smiles a little wanly. Even as her tongue moulds the word, she experiences the familiar embarrassment mingled with shame. But what answer can she give? She is not from anywhere else.

Certainly, she is not prepared for Mrs Van der Hart's response.

Instead of changing the subject or commiserating or getting up and leaving, Mrs Van der Hart says to her: 'Did you know your president is here?'

Dilys pales. She sits up, her back stiff as the cane that she always carried for snakes. Ever so slowly, she swings her head around. 'My president?'

'He is in the same hospital as my husband.'

'What, in Singapore?' she asks. 'Here?'

'He wanted my husband's room, but the hospital wouldn't allow it; he's in the next room, which is smaller,' Mrs Van der Hart says with satisfaction.

Her heart has stopped and her blood is flowing backwards. 'I had no idea he was ill.'

'Well, it can't be too serious, because yesterday he had a tailor in with him,' and before Dilys can ask how in God's name Mrs Van der Hart has come by this information, 'I get it all from Barend, who gets it from the nurses. He's probably just having a service check. Dictators are high maintenance.'

Dilys listens to the gossip passed on by those talkative nurses to Mr Van der Hart. The ban preventing the President from travelling to Europe. The Cuban urologist whom he always insisted on visiting in Kuala Lumpur. The recent transfer of this doctor who has won his trust to a senior position in Singapore – 'where they do things differently. Your president decided to follow him here for treatment, but this being Singapore it means he has to leave all his bodyguards outside, except one, who sleeps on the sofa. Barend found himself standing next to him in the toilet and realised that's who it was.'

But she is standing up and waving. 'There's my daughter. I have to go.'

Over the road – a crocodile line of damp-haired children in white short-sleeved blouses and blue box-pleat belted pinafores.

Dilys studies her long pale fingers that have interlocked as if the future is written in her hands and she can read it. The skin on them is cracked, like a farmer's. Her head tilts back. 'Wait, what hospital did you say?'

'The Stamford – on Arab Street.'

Her palms prickle. 'Which floor?' trying to discipline the excitement that has leaped into her eyes.

Simone led the way along a dark passage, smelling of printer's ink, to a small narrow bathroom adjoining a bedroom. The air was thick and damper than a swamp.

He was lying in a clog-shaped copper bath, naked to the waist. A brown dressing gown was draped across his shoulders and a wet towel wrapped his forehead. Her first impression: his head – crowned with bunched-up tufts of lank black hair – was grotesquely large for his body. Her second: how leathery and inflamed his skin looked. It was the same texture as the knife's sheath.

Balanced across the bath was a pine plank with papers on it and copies of newspapers speckled with drops of bathwater.

Simone retrieved an empty jug from beside the bath and went out, not closing the door.

He was correcting proofs. He reached the end of the paragraph and looked up.

That face. Yellow-grey eyes. A crushed nose. Long sparse hairs for eyebrows. And scabby scales blotching the deformed body. Leprosy had left its rodent's teeth all over his bony shoulders and there was a bitter reek of vinegar that she traced to the towel.

The man in the bath leaned back at an angle. His bloodshot eyes exploring her with Calvinist intensity. Gravely, he assessed her perfect breasts. His eyes grazed over her throat, along her scarf, down her gown. No woman dressed like this, looking like this, had ever stepped into his bathroom.

He indicated with his pen a low stool below the window. She sat, her eyes sweeping the room, taking in more details: the map of their country pinned to the wall; a plate on the windowsill, heaped with sweetbreads.

'Your name again?' asked Marat.

'Charlotte Corday,' she told him, her gloved fingers fidgeting with her lace bodice the only outward sign of nervousness.

'How old are you?' His voice was powerful, melodious; out of keeping with his undeveloped frame.

'Twenty-four.'

He tossed the proofs to the floor. 'Simone says you have come from Caen to see me.'

'That's right.'

The tone in her partner's voice speaking to this beautiful young woman brought Simone back into the bathroom with the jug that she had refilled with water.

She poured him a glass that he raised to his swollen lips. Pieces of almond and ice floated on the surface.

'All right?' his mistress wanted to know.

'You might give it more flavour next time,' grimacing, and handed it back.

She took the empty glass and the untouched plate from the sill. 'I'll heat this up.'

His eyes on the young woman, he nodded and seemed not to notice the door close.

Dilys shakes hands with Mrs Van der Hart as if pumping up water from a long way down. Then she walks back to the Raffles Plaza. The heat from the pavement rises up through her thick skirt, but she does not feel it.

She spends the rest of the morning at the swimming pool on the eighth floor. In the old days, in the days when she was Sleeping Beauty, she would keep her hair above the surface, but she wants to dive under, soak herself. She comes up for air and swims out over the rooftop towards the empty sky and the city. When her fingertips touch the small blue tiles at the other end, she turns and swims in an even breast-stroke, back towards the breakfast bar.

As Dilys finds frequently happens, the act of swimming – like dreaming – releases deeper thoughts. Her mind had stopped at the moment of revelation and now it makes reck-less seesaws to catch up.

– *This coincidence. His presence literally around the corner/my sudden obsession with Charlotte Corday. Isn't it fate speaking?*

– *No, it would be immoral, illegal. Besides, what difference would it make? Look at Iraq after they hanged Saddam Hussein. Look what happened to Charlotte Corday. She was guillotined and reviled and Marat became a martyr.*

– *But if Hitler had died in that suitcase bomb, how many mil-lions of lives would have been saved? Who would suspect a white, middle-class grandmother?*

Up and down she continues. After thirty laps, she climbs out. She knows that she looks a mess, and once she has towelled herself dry she goes down to the lobby to make a hair appointment – it needs a trim anyway. But the earliest they are able to take her is tomorrow morning at 9 a.m. She considers cancelling it, then recalls a hairdresser once telling her that a new haircut can be as good as plastic surgery. She had looked with puzzlement at the pregnant young woman who ran forward to greet her at Heathrow, until she recognised her daughter Rachel beneath the unfamiliar fringe. Dilys's flight doesn't leave until the evening. She confirms the appointment.

It's not yet noon. She feels renewed, less jangled.

Three hours later, Dilys returns to the hotel carrying two large brown paper bags. The swim has sharpened her appetite and once upstairs she orders a steak from the room-service menu. While waiting for it to arrive, she unpacks her new purchases and hangs them up. The smallest item is a laminated identity badge on a chain. She holds it out at arm's length, inspecting it. The lettering is not up to the standard of Miles's printing firm, but from a short distance it convinces. It looks official, she thinks.

Footsteps down the corridor and something squeaking and a rap on the door. A man pushes in a trolley with her meal on it. She has sat down to eat before he is even out of the room.

The steak is minuscule and Dilys plays an antique game from childhood of carving it into smaller and smaller portions to make it last longer. She has picked the plate clean when abruptly she stands up.

She unzips her suitcase and rifles through it for the plastic bag in which she has wrapped the Munch catalogue. Was there a knife in the painting? I'm not sure there was.

Dilys digs out the catalogue and checks the illustration. No, not even a bath. Just two naked figures in a room with a bed. An anonymous room like this one – like the room I'm flying back to, she thinks.

She will never retrieve all the days she sat in a cane chair, not leaving her tiny cement-floored flat back in Africa. Severed, useless, shrunk. The time that was stolen, like the momentous loss of the farm, of her darling Miles – it is unreimbursable.

But does she have the courage to do it herself? In a battle, she can almost imagine killing a figure in the distance with a rifle. Or pushing a button to drop a bomb. But to stab someone ...

Charlotte Corday didn't have a moment of doubt.

'Who taught you to pierce Marat to the heart at first blow?'

'The indignation that filled my own. I was determined to sacrifice my own life in order to save that of my country.'

Dilys picks up the steak knife from the trolley and with the napkin wipes it clean, one side and then the other. Sitting on the edge of her comfortable bed on the twelfth floor of the Raffles Plaza, she remembers the breakfast knives that she kept finding in the kitchen, black with ants. And Beauty leading her out into the chicken yard and reaching an arm into the coop.

Did Charlotte Corday sit in her hotel room and weigh up which part to stab? The heart or throat? His throat would be above the bedclothes; she couldn't bear the horror of pulling back the sheets.

She tests the blade with her thumb and an image of Miles slaughtering a springbok flashes before her. The neck tautened back, the swift slash of the sharpened blade, the bright spurts of blood on the tobacco-coloured earth.

'This is how you do it, Mrs Hoskins,' Beauty had said, holding up the chicken like a lantern.

She drops it with a clatter onto the plate and goes into the bathroom. Coming back out, she changes into her nightdress. But she is not able to leave the steak knife alone. Once more she walks over to the trolley and picks it up. Hadn't she managed to put that cow out of its misery – the bulging, all-seeing eyes meeting hers, knowing what she was about to do, and after she had done it a whistling sound as awful in its way as the last sound that she would hear bubbling out of Miles's mouth.

Dilys looks around the room, her eyes settling on the bed. She decides to try the knife out on the pillows. But when she raises it, something in her resists doing damage to the hotel's Italian linen. It remains suspended at a ridiculous angle in the cooled air above her pillow.

And lowers her arm.

She weighs the knife one last time in her hand. Then she tucks it between the pages of the catalogue as if to mark a place and lies down on the bed.

'So what is happening in Caen?'

She tells him.

'You have the names of those involved?' He takes up his pen, waiting.

She dictates. It's a roll-call of her friends. Barbaroux, Buzot, Guadet, Louvet, Pétion ... Her voice is even, without strain. Summoning them to her side.

He writes down the names, licking something from his tongue, followed by what sounds like a titter. In his excitement, the dressing gown slips further from his shoulders, exposing something ghastly.

She leans forward, suppressing a little cough, and her hand delves into her bodice.

'I will have them guillotined in a few days.' Less than two yards away, the pen hovers. 'Is that the lot?'

She leaps up, toppling the stool, withdraws the knife from its sheath, and in a single downward movement plunges it sideways into his chest. She skewers it in deeper, through veins and tendons. He has no time to respond, save with an exhalation of air as the steel tip punctures his lung. She pushes in harder, into his heart, until only the ebony handle protrudes.

The squelching sound when she pulls out the knife is not unlike a pumpkin hitting the earth. The blood jets up – over her wrist, her bare snowy neck – through a wound in the top of his chest that will be wide enough for Simone to fit her fingertips into.

He shouts out, but it is not his voice that is heard by the women who slam open the door. It is Charlotte's scream.

Dilys goes one more time into the bathroom to check that her lipstick is not too dark. She has had her hair done in the salon downstairs and is wearing a blouse of ivory silk open at the neck and a conservative foresty green skirt. She might be on her way to the Kennel Club Show.

Anyone who looked closer, though, would see the eraser marks. Children gone, husband dead – now it's just her. A woman left behind who has had to watch everyone leave. Her unresolvable fury is aimed as much at the President as towards her loneliness.

Her body tenses, as if it has heard one of Miles's favourite milongas strike up. She runs her tongue over her lips and murmurs to her spectacled face in the mirror: 'Don't worry, darling.'

She inclines her head and very carefully slips the chain over it, tucking the laminated badge down into her cleavage. The owner of the family-run print-shop in the Funan Centre had given her a good price to have it made up, even throwing in the chain for free. It was another of Miles's beliefs. 'If you've got an identity badge round your neck, people won't stop you.'

She returns to the room and gulps down the gin and tonic that she mixed herself from the mini-bar. She is no longer afraid. She picks up her bag from the bed and plucks the plastic room-card from the wall socket, extinguishing the lights, and leaves.

The Stamford Hospital is but a short walk from her hotel. She gets through surprisingly easily. 'I'm visiting Mr Van der Hart,' she tells a harassed-looking receptionist. Before the young woman has time to formulate a reply, Dilys's face takes on the expression of blunt intransigence that so annoys her children. 'Ward C,' she says.

'Are you a relation?'

'I've brought him another book,' Dilys explains in a triumphant maternal voice. The sound in her chest as she walks through the lift is like the tail of a dog beating on the carpet.

Afterword

COFFEE-PICKING IS ALL ABOUT THE RED BERRIES. The green ones aren't ready yet. The black ones have gone bad and missed their chance. It's the red ones that matter. The ones the shape of gooseberries and the colour of cherries. They're the ones that are good to go. They're the ones with the just-right coffee beans in, two in each berry, side by side. They're the ones that end up in your cup.

And they're the ones that have brought new hope and a new future to the people of Macala in Honduras. Come harvest time, the scene in this mountain village looks much the same as it has for generations. People still head to the fields under a sun too new to banish the early-morning chills. They still work their way through head-high coffee plants, tossing berries into wicker baskets tied to their waists until the falling sun makes it impossible to tell good from bad. And they still lay the beans out on large sheets to dry, raking them now and again and covering them at night to avoid the damp. Coffee, people here will tell you, is only coffee if it's dried naturally, under the sun.

But while the process of tending the earth has changed little over time, the lives that many families in Macala live because of the earth have altered completely. Most people here rely on farming to earn a living. Many of them used to struggle to get by, earning very little for a lot of effort. But because of the determination of a small group of people the future has become a source of hope, rather than fear.

Things began to change around a decade ago, when a group of women got together and decided enough was enough. Tired of working tiny plots of land for very little return, and sick of the domestic violence many of them were experiencing, they began running workshops, discussing what women could do to earn more and put themselves on an equal footing with men. As people listened and started getting involved, the women made efforts to learn and share new skills. They found out more about farming and how to get the most out of the land. They organised sessions on things like bookkeeping and business administration. With confidence growing, people started to believe that they had the power to change their lives.

Oxfam got involved and began offering support a few years later, enabling the women – who work as a co-operative – to buy land, which they farmed together. They began growing a bigger variety of crops and selling them more widely, for a better price. Ten years on, the co-operative has more than 250 members. They grow grains, vegetables and aloe vera products, as well as Fair Trade coffee, which is now exported around the world.

It's an inspiring story, and a revealing one. With a little investment and a lot of resolve, the local community has been rejuvenated. Many more people now have a reliable source of income. Men and women are working more closely together, and women have more confidence to stand up to violence. There are less obvious consequences, too. More children are in school, because their parents no longer need them to work to earn extra money. And people are able to eat a more balanced, more nutritious diet. It's an incredible, wide-ranging turnaround, and one that's come from the ground. From the earth.

At Oxfam, we talk a lot about the 'right to a sustainable livelihood'. It's essentially the right to a decent job, a safe place to call home, clean water in your cup and enough food on your plate. The basics, in other words. Except that, for a lot of people, they're not.

And that's why projects like this one in Honduras are so valuable. They help people to see their rights become a reality, to get the basics and start building on them. We work on similar projects around the world, listening to people's ideas and offering whatever support works best in each situation.

So in Tanzania, we're working to help farmers grow drought-resistant rice. It's a simple idea, based on learning new farming techniques, but it means people can rely on a better income, even if they can't rely on the rain. In southern India, we're working with cotton growers as they start to use organic methods. They no longer need to rack up huge debts paying for expensive, dangerous pesticides, their land is now in better condition, and their yields are improving. In north-eastern Brazil, where keeping livestock is tough, we're supporting people as they turn to bee-keeping instead. And, in Ethiopia, we're helping people with negotiating skills, so they can push to get the best possible price for their goods.

In all of these projects, the thinking is the same. Work with small farmers, and big results follow. With practical training and investment in basic services and infrastructure, people in rural areas start getting more from the ground. By working together, they can negotiate more effectively and earn more. And, as incomes grow, the benefits ripple through communities and beyond.

Other parts of local economies, not just agriculture, start to prosper. People who previously struggled to make themselves heard – often women and people without land – get involved and begin to find a voice. The push for better schools and medical services begins, diets improve, and so on and so on. Soon enough, agriculture becomes the catalyst for change on a much wider scale. And in places like Colombia and Mali, where we're working with tens of thousands of farmers on projects like these, that means a profound ripple effect.

Three-quarters of the world's poorest people live in rural areas. So when we get to grips with rural poverty, the world will start to look very different. But government support and aid money for agriculture has been falling for years – and what support there is hasn't focused on small farmers.

At the same time, the climate has already started to change. With the weather in many places getting more unpredictable, farmers face new challenges. Challenges that can be met – by growing drought-resistant rice, for example – but not ignored. That's why, at the same time as focusing on places like Macala, we keep pushing governments to recognise the huge role small-scale agriculture has in the fight against poverty. It's also one of the reasons climate change is now central to our work.

There are thousands of places like Macala. Thousands of places where people are already thriving in tough conditions. And there are millions of people who, given the right support, will follow Macala's lead. There's no doubting the difference that small-scale farming can make. All that's needed is leadership. It's time to make the earth move, for everyone.

oxfam.org.uk/development

Oxfam

Be Humankind